SPIN THE BOTTLE

PARTY GAMES

RHIAN CAHILL

Spin the Bottle
A Party Games Novel
By Rhian Cahill

For more information visit:
www.rhiancahill.com

To all those who have spun the bottle a time or two.
To Heidi, for your never-ending patience, understanding and support.
As always, for the man who goes after my dreams with as much passion as I do. Together forever, babe.

1

MACKENZIE STOOD JUST inside the front door—briefcase in one hand, handle of his wheeled bag in the other—and stared at all the strangers in his house. Not strangers exactly, some of the faces were very well known, but they weren't his friends, or acquaintances for that matter.

"I'll kill her." The words rumbled through his lips on a harsh breath and were completely drowned out by the throbbing beat of the torturous mash-up the DJ was playing.

From where he stood, Mac could see the guy standing in the far corner of the living room surrounded by state-of-the-art equipment. Dressed in baggy clothes, with a multitude of gold jewellery, dark glasses and dreadlocks dripping off his head, the man was a stark reminder of why the club scene no longer appealed.

Mac curled his fingers tighter around his bag handles as he scanned the crowd to no avail. She was nowhere to be seen. With a growl, he turned and headed for the stairs. He took them two at a time, his ears ringing and his heart pounding, whether from anger at her latest effort to annoy him or the horrible mix of music assaulting the walls, he didn't know. Upstairs proved difficult to navigate with a line of scantily clad women queuing for the bathroom. Trying not to bash his luggage into any of them, he wove his way towards his room.

He avoided eye contact and ignored the suggestive comments. Halfway along the corridor something brushed over his arse and his steps faltered. Unsure if he'd been felt up or not, he kept moving, but a definite pinch to one butt cheek had him jerking and quickening his pace. Mac wasn't about to stop and confront anyone. He wanted to reach the safety of his room before any of the vultures managed to get her claws into him. He knew the type—rich, spoilt and totally self-absorbed.

Mac had learned his lesson about those kinds of females very early in life. Watching the plastic, shallow creatures fawn all over his best friend for most of their lives had certainly opened his eyes to the many pitfalls of the female gender. Toss in Lachlan's step-mother, and Mackenzie considered himself an expert on the numerous wiles of women. Reaching the end of the hall, he wrapped his hand around the door knob and breathed a sigh of relief as he entered his room, shut the door behind him and flipped the lock.

He strode across the thick carpeted floor, the muffled noise from the party grating on his nerves. His bedside clock read seven fifteen, and he clenched his jaw, grinding his molars together. *Dammit*. After the hellish week he'd had he wanted to sit back with a cold beer and enjoy a nice night with a few friends. Lilli had promised she'd only invite a couple of people. A couple? *Hah!* More like a couple hundred. With a grunt of frustration, Mac tossed his briefcase on the bed and made his way to the bathroom, carryon in tow.

The racket from below lessened as he entered his white and blue tiled en suite and he closed the door to further block out the sound. Mac unzipped his bag, retrieved his toiletries kit and put it on the counter. He lifted the lid on the laundry hamper and piled in a week's worth of dirty clothes, then reached into the shower recess and turned on the water. While the downpour warmed, he kicked off his shoes and socks, stripped out of his shirt and pants and dropped the clothing in the basket beside him. Steam billowed out and he quickly grabbed what he needed from his kit and stepped under the hot spray.

Mac leaned his head back and let the hard cascade of water wash away some of his tension. His shoulders were bunched tight, whether from the anger over Lilli's latest stunt or from the hum of arousal that always buzzed through him when he thought of her, he couldn't be sure. He tried to ignore his body's reactions and popped open the shampoo bottle. Mechanically, he dealt with cleaning away the day's grime while he pushed thoughts of Lillian McDermott from his mind. She was the one woman he couldn't afford to think about while naked and wet.

Lillian McDermott. *Lilli*.

His best friend's little sister. The last female on earth he should want, and yet he did—had for too many years to count. If Lachlan knew the fantasies Mac had about Lilli, he'd kill him, which was only one of the reasons to stop his train of thought. Turning, Mac twisted the hot tap off and stood under the cold spray in an attempt to freeze the heat Lillian inspired. Not that he ever managed to completely eradicate it with Lilli around, but he could certainly get it under control enough to stop from doing anything stupid.

Like last time?

With a groan, Mac closed his eyes and pressed his forehead to the wall. Cold water pelted his back and slid down his spine, but the chill didn't register. His mind had rewound to seven months ago. Seven months, three days to be exact. Not that he was counting. The memory of that day remained as fresh as though he'd lived it just hours earlier. It was his Groundhog Day moment. He couldn't begin to count the number of times he'd relived those few minutes.

It was rare for them to be alone in the house but Lachlan had received a summons from his father, and regardless of the older man no longer holding the reins of the family's media empire or his friend's life, Lachlan had gone. Roland's recent diagnosis of Alzheimer's had softened all their views towards the once-tyrannical family patriarch. So Mac and Lilli ate dinner without his best friend as a shield, talked about unimportant things, and Mac actually believed his desire for Lilli was under control. Fat chance. He had no clue when it was that things had changed. When she'd gone from being his best friend's little sister to the woman he wanted above all others. All he knew was he had to keep his hands off. Which was easier said than done.

One second he'd been in control, the next Lilli was in his arms, their mouths joined in the most erotic kiss of his life. Soft, pliant lips gave way, and he slipped his tongue inside to taste more of her. A hint of spice from their meal and the sweetness of her cocktail enticed him deeper. Mac slanted his lips across hers and their tongues collided in a frenzy of want and need. The combination of chili and strawberry daiquiri lingered on her tongue, the fiery-sweet flavour the perfect symbol of their scorching kiss. Wicked innocence.

Mac's body tightened. Lust coiled hot and hungry in his balls. His cock lengthened—hardened as his pulse pounded through his veins. He sucked in a breath of damp air and reached for his cock. Lightning shot through him at the memory of her hands touching him.

Lilli skimmed her splayed hands across his chest, over his shoulders and down his back—her fingers burning him through his shirt, her nails scoring his skin. He ground his hips to hers, his hard-on pressing against her stomach. She moaned into his mouth as she pushed back, her lower body rocking into his. Mac gripped her arse, pulled her up on her toes and fit their bodies together in perfect alignment to drive them both wild.

He'd gone too far, remembered too much, and past experience told him he'd need to relieve the pressure with his own hand and the vivid recollection of Lilli's mouth under his, her body pressed to his. Mac tightened his grip, pulled his cock harder as his orgasm drew closer.

She tangled her fingers in his hair, tugged on the short strands and sent shivers down his spine. He squeezed her arse as he worked his fingertips towards her pussy. Lilli wrapped her legs around his waist and the short skirt she wore rode up her thighs, exposed the part of her he sought. Heat and moisture met his skin, the thin barrier of her underwear no match for the hot need flowing from her core.

Mac's harsh breaths and pounding heart echoed in his ears. He worked his cock harder, ran his thumb over the swollen tip, his precome easing the slide of his fingers. His sac tightened, tucking his balls close to his body as release approached.

He pressed the silky cloth under his fingers into her slit, parted her folds and searched for her clit in spite of the barrier. The hard knot of nerves stood tall, pulsed beneath his touch. She rocked against him, thrusting back onto his hand, forward onto his cock. His mouth left hers to trail kisses along her jaw while he continued to torture her sex with his hand. Mac nipped at her ear, sucked the lobe into his mouth and flicked it with his tongue.

His hand moved faster.

Lilli's hips bucked and more cream soaked her undies. He cursed the obstacle between them, wanted to feel her slick, wet flesh on his skin. Wanted to slide his fingers through her folds and thrust them inside her. Drive them deep and find her G-spot, stroke her inside and out until she screamed his name.

"Mac."

She rippled against him, her orgasm sneaking up on both of them as she bucked and thrashed in his arms. Heat and wetness coated his hand. Lilli buried her face in the side of his neck as she rode out the last waves of her release.

Mac pumped his shaft with firm, punishing strokes. His balls tightened and his spine tingled. He shouted Lilli's name with the first spasm, groaned on the second. With each contraction, a thick rope of semen spilled from his cock, the liquid hot on his skin as it coated his hand. As he came down, he remembered the rest and cursed himself for the bastard he was.

A door slammed and Lachlan's voice boomed through the house. Mac pushed Lilli away, dropped her to her feet and stepped back. Her face was flushed and covered in a sheen of sweat. His balls ached, throbbed with the need to finish what he'd started. Footsteps echoed behind him.

"Shit. That was bad. Very, very bad," he murmured.

Her eyes widened, filled with moisture, and her trembling fingers came up to cover her mouth.

"Hey! Where is everyone?" *Lachlan yelled from the front of the house.*

Lilli gasped. Her gaze darted over his shoulder before she *glanced back at him. She shook her head and then spun on her heel and ran from the room.*

"Fuck."

His fist slammed into the shower wall. Pain ricochet through his hand and up his arm, but he welcomed it. After what he'd done, it was the least he deserved. For the millionth time, he questioned his actions—his lack of them. He'd let her go that night, hadn't had much choice when Lachlan entered the kitchen. It wasn't until Mac went looking for Lilli the next morning and discovered her gone that he'd really thought about what had happened and what a fuckwit he'd been. His best friend really would kill him if he knew the sordid details of his encounter with Lilli.

Mac leaned into the wall and sighed. He'd tried to fix it. He'd followed her to New York only to be turned away from the closed-door photo shoot where he'd tracked her down. She'd avoided him ever since. She never answered his calls, left messages with his secretary instead of ringing him directly. He pushed off the wall and switched off the water. There was grovelling to be done, but he couldn't do it when she avoided him. The one consolation of this party was Lillian McDermott could be relied on to be the perfect hostess, therefore she wouldn't hide out in her room. Tonight, she wouldn't escape him.

LIL SURVEYED the room with a satisfied smile. The party was a smash hit and it wasn't even eight o'clock. Still plenty of hours left in Friday night for everyone to enjoy the unique theme she'd chosen. *Are You Game?* was the brainchild of her high school friend, Cassandra Moreland. The company specialised in party games for all occasions, and recently Cassie had decided to branch out into the adult party arena. Lil had jumped at the chance to be her friend's first customer.

Cassie walked through the crowd, checking game stations on her way across the room to where Lil stood. Her friend paused next to a man in a tight, black T-shirt, the words *Are You Game?* in blood-red across his impressive chest. He said something close to Cassie's ear that made her friend laugh and left a smile on her lips as she walked away. The room was full to bursting with people, and more came in and out to see what game had been set up. Each room on the lower level of the house had a different game in it. Some seemed bland enough, but it was the adult twist Cassie had given each one that turned them from innocent to scandalous.

"It's going great," Lil said as Cassie reached her side.

"Yes, but I think the guests help. They're in the mood to party so anything goes. Besides, you've got an open bar and most of them are on their way to being smashed already." Cassie smiled as she scanned the room once more.

"What are you looking for? You just walked through checking everything."

"Have to keep your eye on the ball. Something could go wrong at any moment, and it's my job to make sure nothing ruins your party." She turned to look at Lil. "I take my job very seriously, even when the client is a friend and doing me a very big favour."

"I was more than happy to be your first." Lil grinned. "Besides, it's not often I get free rein of the house without either Mackenzie or Lachlan around to nag about what I'm doing."

"I thought you said they were due in tonight?"

"Mac's plane doesn't land until after nine, and I'm not sure about Lachlan. No one in his office could give me a definite answer, and as usual he's not answering his phone. It won't matter because by the time either of them arrives it'll be too late to stop the fun."

Cassie shook her head. "Why do you do that?"

"What?"

"You know what." Cassie gripped Lil's hand. "You're not the supermodel party girl you pretend to be. I don't understand why you go out of your way to project this superficial image while you hide who you really are."

Lil sighed. She couldn't explain it, this compulsion to live up—or down—to everyone's expectations. It all started with her mother, but then didn't every child blame their parents? She shrugged. "It's what they expect."

"And what about what you expect? What you want?"

"I'm getting it. This is only a small part of my life, Cassie, you know that." Lil squeezed her friend's hand. "I'm done with this world after tonight. This party is my big hurrah."

"You're quitting?"

"Shh." Lil glanced around to check no one had heard her friend. She leaned close to whisper in her friend's ear. "I quit. Months ago actually. This last job was personal."

"Are you going to make an announcement?" Cassie asked.

"No. I was planning..." Lil's gaze snagged on a head of tousled blond hair across the room. *Mackenzie.* "Oh shit. Gotta go. Talk later." She turned and fled before Cassie could say another word.

Weaving through the partygoers, Lil quickly made her way out of the room. She glanced over her shoulder as she cleared the doorway. Mac was no longer in sight and she breathed a sigh of relief, but she wasn't taking any chances so kept moving. What was he doing home already? His flight wasn't due in until ten past nine. She'd double-checked this afternoon with his secretary to be sure he wouldn't arrive before the party was well underway. Dammit. The last thing she needed was an angry Mac in her face.

She headed for the kitchen. If she could manage to dodge him for a few hours... Oh, who was she kidding? He'd be pissed off no matter how much time passed. He wouldn't let her small fib about the size of the guest list go without a lecture. Lil checked on the food supply only to discover one of Cassie's staff had it under control. Waiters and waitresses made their way back and forth to the party rooms with trays of finger food. Everything ran with smooth efficiency and Lil had no doubt her friend could run a country with as much skill and make it look easy.

Nothing had been left to chance, every detail checked and double-checked by a member of Cassie's team. So far Lillian hadn't done a thing, and from what she'd seen over the last two hours, it wasn't likely she would all night. Which was good, because this was her farewell bash, of course no one knew that but her and her closest friend, Cameron. And now Cassie. Why she'd let that bit of information slip was beyond her. She'd had no intention of telling anyone anything. Her plan had been to fade quietly into oblivion, and as long as she didn't let her tongue get away from her the rest of the evening, she'd still be able to pull that off.

Lil smiled. The thought of finally doing what she'd always wanted gave her butterflies in the pit of her stomach, but all the years she'd sacrificed to a modelling career she had no taste for had paid off. Her bank account looked healthy even with the big chunk she'd used to start up her Lilli Pond label of children's clothing. Of course, this last twelve months of being in the black meant she no longer had to model to earn money. She glanced around the kitchen once more as she headed out into the dining room.

"Lillian, darling."

The smile slid from Lil's mouth. There was no mistaking that high-pitched voice. Plastering on her game face, she turned to greet the woman Lillian was one hundred percent positive had not received an invite to the party.

"Chantal." One look at the man on the other woman's arm told Lil how she'd found out about this evening. "Aaron, so lovely to see you both." She wasn't sure why she'd invited Aaron after the way he'd leaked the photos of her sunbathing topless at his private estate. A long history of friendship and politeness seemed the only reason, but he'd just guaranteed himself no further niceties from her.

Chantal leaned forward and delivered air kisses to either side of Lil's face. A cloud of nasal-clogging perfume threatened to choke her, and Lil tried not to cough.

"I'm assuming my invite got caught up in the mail, Lillian. If it wasn't for Aaron here, I wouldn't have known a thing about your party."

There was no love lost between them and Lil had no intention of letting Australia's latest starlet think otherwise. "I never sent you one, Chantal. I had no idea you were out of rehab yet." She'd raised her voice just enough to be heard by the people around them and a second of gasped silence held them all for a moment.

Aaron flinched as Chantal's talon-like nails dug into his arm. Chantal narrowed her baby blues, leaned forward and spoke through clenched teeth. "I wasn't in rehab. I was involved in a car accident and spent time in the hospital recovering from my injuries."

As a cover story, it wasn't bad, not that anyone inside the industry believed it, but the general public pretty much took gossip mags as gospel. Lil had no doubt the press were being fed exactly what Chantal's management wanted them to print.

"I'm glad to see you're fully recovered. If you'll both excuse me, I need to speak with the party organiser." Lil turned and pushed her way through the growing crowd. With any luck, she wouldn't cross paths with Chantal again. Why the other woman had made them sworn enemies still eluded her, but Lillian wasn't about to let it spoil tonight. She'd have Chantal removed before it came to that.

Lillian paused in the doorway to the living room. The hired DJ had set up in the far corner with a number of wireless speakers strategically placed around the house so that every room could be blasted with music. Cassie had explained that the volume would be turned down once the games really got going, but for the first few hours the loud beat of the latest hit songs would be played. There wasn't a game set up in this room yet, but Lil knew Cassie had planned for an adult version of musical chairs. She couldn't wait to see what kind of twist her friend had put on a childhood favourite.

"Hey, Lil."

She turned to see Mac's brother, Alec, heading her way. Glancing around, she made sure Mac wasn't with him. "Hi, Alec, glad you could make it."

"Um, this isn't exactly what I expected." He dragged his hand through his too-long blond hair. "Mac said a few friends, some food and a couple of beers."

"Well, Mac was wrong. Besides, it's my party not his, and when did you talk to him about it?" Lil asked, curious to know when Mac had found the time to speak to Alec seeing how he hadn't tried to ring her in two days. Not that she would have answered his call.

"He rang me from Melbourne just before he boarded an earlier flight."

Damn. No wonder he was already here. "I didn't know he'd changed his plans."

"I was a little distracted, but I think he mentioned working with idiots and having had enough." Alec laughed. "I guess he bashed some heads and came home early. Although I'm not sure he'd be happy to be home with all this going on. He was pretty adamant it would be a quiet evening relaxing with close friends. His description was what convinced me to come."

"Sorry, it was never going to be a quiet gathering, but please don't go." She could see Alec wanted to leave. "I saw Mac before, so he's around here somewhere. Why don't you grab a beer and go find him. I'm sure you've got some catching up to do." Lil nudged him farther into the house, towards the bar.

"I promised I'd show so I need to at least talk to him, I guess."

"Yes, you know Mac will never let it go if you don't at least find him." She gave Alec another push just as she spotted a familiar blond head. "Go, enjoy. I'll catch you later."

Lil turned in the direction of the backyard. She greeted people as she passed but didn't linger. She had to put as much distance between her and Mac as possible. Each room Lil looked into appeared more packed with bodies than the last, and Cassie gave her two thumbs-up and a wave as they passed on either side of the kitchen. The huge games room led to the back deck and the full wall of open sliding doors let in a light evening breeze, but it wasn't enough to cool things down. Summer in Sydney had been a scorcher, and today had hit the high thirties with minimal reprieve when the sun went down.

The air was warm and sticky already, and with the house packed full of laughing, talking, drinking partiers, things were heating up fast. Lillian checked the control panel and switched the air conditioning down a few degrees. It wouldn't be as effective with all the doors and windows open, but she'd take all the air circulation she could get. A game of twenty-one started up in the corner and Lil watched as everyone was dealt cards. The first guy busted and picked up a shot glass filled with clear liquid, probably tequila, and swallowed it in one gulp.

Each player, one after the other, took a card. All of them went above twenty-one and took a shot. A second round started up quickly and Lil stood off to the side to watch. She was enjoying the game when someone pressed into the back of her. Thinking the person wanted to get past, she stepped forward only to be stopped by an arm around her waist, a strong grip that pulled her back against the solid hot wall of muscle behind her.

Warm air fanned over her ear and neck, sending shivers down her spine. His scent filled her nose, and he didn't need to speak for Lil to know who had hold of her. Mac. He gripped her hip, splayed his fingers and urged her to take a step backwards. Her body was never her own when he was around, and she let him lead her where he willed. He moved them out of the way and stepped them into the corner of the room.

In a second, Mac spun her around. He pushed her into the corner and caged her in, his hands flat on the wall either side of her waist. In her five-inch heels they were eye to eye and she could see the swirl of emotion in his blue gaze. She'd gone too far with tonight's party, but that wasn't what had her worried. No, what made her anxious was the look on his face that said he wanted to kiss her. They'd been there and done that with disastrous effects. Lillian didn't know if she could survive a second time.

"You can run, Lilli, but you can't hide forever."

2

MAC WAITED FOR THE EXPLOSION. He didn't for one second think she'd let him get away with pinning her in a corner. No, Lillian McDermott never let anyone limit her. She took what she wanted when she wanted. It galled him to think she'd turned out exactly like her mother. That woman had a lot to answer for, the least of which was her absentee parenting. He shuddered. The last person he wanted occupying his mind was Gabriella McDermott. He'd much rather concentrate on her sexy daughter.

The one who drove him nuts but pulled him closer with every breath he took. He'd tried to stay away, tried to ignore the gut-burning need to see if the kiss they'd shared was a fluke. His gaze dropped to her mouth. Slightly parted, her cherry-red lips beckoned, a siren's call he knew he couldn't refuse—didn't want to deny. Mac leaned forward, his lips a breath from hers.

"Mac?"

His name on her tongue, the puff of warm air that blew over his chin and the tremor of her lips made him smile. "Lilli."

"What are you doing?" she whispered.

"I thought that was obvious." He didn't pull away but moved his body closer to hers, his chest barely touching the tips of her breasts when she sucked in a breath.

"You can't."

"Can't?"

"N-no." Her lips brushed his. "It's bad, remember?"

Mac pulled back a fraction to focus on her eyes. "What?"

"Kissing me." She licked her lips and sent his blood pressure soaring. "When we did it before, you said it was bad."

For a second, he hadn't a clue what she meant, and then it clicked. "Oh, no, it wasn't the kiss that was bad, Lilli." He lowered his head, brought his mouth back within touching distance of hers. "I'll prove it."

He slanted his mouth across hers. Thrust his tongue between her parted lips to plunder. Mac didn't ease into the kiss. He dove deep, headfirst. She tasted of champagne and cherries. Of lush decadence that spoke of untold pleasure. The party faded away, lost in the mating of their mouths. Nothing existed but the woman now in his arms, her body plastered to his, her soft curves cradling his hard edges as he devoured her.

Her breath hitched when he sucked on her tongue, and the gaspy little moan that followed the caress of his hand down her spine dragged him further into the most sublime kiss of his life. His cock throbbed, his balls ached and every nerve ending sizzled with the need to take her.

Here.

Now.

Against the wall.

Mac pushed his hand beneath the hem of her too-short dress, palmed her bare arse cheek and squeezed. Her supple flesh filled his hand, her smooth skin like silk under his fingertips. Jesus, she either wore a thong or nothing at all. Both options had his pulse accelerating and his cock stiffening. Blood rushed through his veins, pounded in his ears and slammed his heart against his rib cage. Lilli's fingers tangled in his hair and tugged. The sting of pain was an erotic thrill he never dreamed would turn him on.

Someone bumped into his back hard enough to make him stumble. He pulled his mouth from hers and let her go to brace his arms on the wall, shielding her body with his. She stared at him, eyes wide, her pupils dilated and those cherry-red lips wet from his kisses. A shudder rippled through him, the sight of her flushed cheeks and rosy mouth injecting another burst of lust into his system. This wasn't the time or the place, but damn if he could get himself to care.

Her nipples were hard nubs digging into his chest and her breath came in harsh pants, mirroring his. Mac fought for some of his legendary control. Where had a lifetime's worth of discipline disappeared to? What was it about sweet, innocent Lilli that cut the reins of restraint he'd lived by? He looked down at her, the skin-tight black dress she wore contradicted the idea of sweet innocence, but something about the provocative outfit didn't ring true, he just couldn't put his finger on why not.

She gained her wits before he did. Mac was still breathing hard and ogling her cleavage when she ducked beneath his outstretched arm and escaped him. Trapped in a lust-induced fog, it took him a moment to realise she'd gone. When he did, he lowered his head and cursed himself a fool. For the second time, he'd had her in his arms and let her get away. That stopped here and now. If their first kiss all those months ago hadn't convinced him, this second one had. Lilli would be his, body and soul, he would own her before the night was done. It was only fair. After all, she'd owned him from the moment his body had begun to crave hers.

"Hey, Mac, there you are."

Mac glanced over his shoulder to see his brother a few feet

away. "Hey, Alec." He took a deep breath and turned to face Alec.

"Not exactly the party you mentioned."

"No." The word sounded more like a growl than speech.

"I take it you weren't privy to the plans," Alec said with a smile on his lips.

"No." Again with the growling.

Alec looked at him with one eyebrow raised. "You all right?"

Mac clenched his fists, his short nails digging into the soft flesh of his palms. He needed to get control of his emotions or Alec would be asking questions he wasn't ready to answer. "Yeah, tough week at work, and I'm ready for a little down time not a raging party."

"I'm with you on that."

"Have you signed that contract yet?" Mac asked.

"Don't start on that again, Mac. You know how I feel about it."

"Alec, don't be stupid. This is the biggest thing that will ever come your way." Mac couldn't fathom anyone turning down the offer a major US celebrity had extended to his brother, but as usual, Alec walked to the beat of his own drum.

"Come on, Mac, I'm not star material. I like getting dirty, and dirt doesn't look so good on TV." Alec brought the bottle of beer in his hand to his lips and took a sip. "Besides, I've got enough money to see me comfortable the rest of my life. I don't need any more."

"It isn't about money. It's about success."

"See, that's where you're missing the point completely. And pissing me off. Right now I'm a thousand times more successful than I ever dreamed I'd be. I'm happy, content and nothing can make my life any better than it is. Not a contract from some American big shot. Not..." Alec's gaze followed someone across the room. "Look, I'm done talking about his. I need another beer. I'll catch ya before I head out."

Before Mac could argue further, his brother disappeared into the growing crowd. He scanned the many faces in the room, most were familiar, a few not. He spotted their neighbours in the far corner talking to a redhead he'd never laid eyes on before. A shout from the group playing cards drew his gaze and he watched as three of the players threw their cards in the centre of the table and downed shots of tequila. This party might not be his thing, but he had to hand it to Lilli, she knew how to have fun and she'd certainly made sure everyone here tonight had a great time.

He pushed off the wall with a sigh and went in search of a beer. If he was going to be stuck with all these people in his house, he may as well get something out of it. And if he managed to corner Lilli again, he'd do more than kiss her. Of course he'd have to make sure they were in a room without any onlookers. He wasn't into exhibitionism, even if her choice of career suggested she was. No, when he got his hands on her again it would be just the two of them.

THE ONLY PROBLEM with being the hostess was everyone wanted a piece of you. Lillian extricated herself from another conversation and searched for Cameron. Where had the woman gone? She's been right beside her a second ago. At least her friend had put in an appearance. Lil had known the lure of meeting Lachlan would be too much for Cam to resist, and she'd used him like the proverbial carrot on a stick to convince Cam to show. It didn't matter how much the other woman pretended disinterest, Lil knew otherwise. Over the years,

Cameron Winters had developed a sight-unseen crush on Lillian's big brother.

Lil couldn't help the smile that curled her lips. Cameron's interest may have been sparked by years of candid conversation, but Lachlan's interest went all the way back to a teenage boy's lust for the woman voted sexiest on the planet. Kole— Cameron's former modeling persona. Lillian had clear memories of the poster on the wall in her brother's bedroom. It was the reason she'd felt so at home with Cam on her first photo shoot. She'd never met the other woman until that day, and finding herself in an unfamiliar world, Lillian had gravitated to the only familiar face. They'd come away from that first job with a solid working relationship and a friendship that would last a lifetime.

She wanted Cameron to see the proofs for the Golden Lilli ad campaign before the other woman came up with an excuse to flee the crowded party. Cam's photography skills were legendary, but Lil was pretty sure the woman had outdone herself this time. She wanted to get her friend's thoughts before giving final approval. Lillian ducked out into the foyer and spotted Cam on the stairs a second before she spied Mac and Lachlan heading her way. *Shit.* When had Lachlan arrived? She slipped behind a set of broad shoulders and hid until they'd passed.

Peeking out from her hiding spot, Lil watched as her brother and his best friend were swallowed up by the mass of designer-label-clad bodies moving about the house. She was just about to go in the opposite direction when Cam rushed by. Lillian wasn't surprised to see her friend following Lachlan, and as much as she could do without another run-in with Mac, Lil found herself treading the same path as the others. The two men wove their way through the crush of bodies with ease. They stopped at regular intervals to talk. Unable to hear the conversation between them, Lil used her years of experience observing their friendship to determine her brother was pissed off and his best friend was taunting him mercilessly.

Mac pointed at the game of Twister currently being played in the library and both of them moved closer. Cam followed and Lillian edged into the room behind her. Lil quickly manoeuvred her way through the people watching the game set up in the middle of the floor. When Mac offered Lachlan as the next player, Lil held her breath. But her brother didn't object and the game in progress continued until the well-known television host dropped to the floor ending the round. There was some nervous chatter and a smart-ass comment or two, but all eyes remained on Lachlan. The room frozen in place as everyone waited nervously for him to make a move.

Lachlan broke the spell. "I think you won," he said to the young woman whose body was contorted above the plastic mat and her downed challenger.

A recent *Australian's Got Talent* winner, she blushed and giggled like a schoolgirl before collecting an article of clothing from the TV weatherman in charge of the spinner. As one, the room held their breath when the reporter asked Lachlan to ante up a piece of clothing to play. No one was more surprised than Lillian when he whipped off his shirt and handed it over. Lil knew her brother took care of himself, but the murmurs of approval from the women around her opened her eyes to him in a whole new way. He could easily grace the pages of one of his own fashion magazines.

Lillian watched Cam move closer, and with the skill only a once-world-renowned supermodel could manage, remove her bra without revealing herself to the room. Lil didn't need to wait for Cam to move to know what would happen next. Her friend was about to challenge her brother to a game. She had no clue what her friend had in mind, and she wasn't sure Cam had even thought it through, but as the flimsy black strips of cloth changed hands there was no turning back.

Like everyone else, Lillian stood mesmerised as tension arced between Cam and Lachlan. Her brother looked ready to tear Cameron apart, while Cam eyed Lachlan as though he were a smorgasbord and she hadn't eaten in a month. Neither appeared willing to back down, and Lil waited for the fireworks to begin. The spin of the arrow started the game. Lost in the couple waging war on a Twister mat, she didn't notice the person edging closer to her until it was too late.

Lillian knew who it was the second he touched her. *Mac.* The familiar feel and scent of him were imbedded in every cell of her being, branded like the signature of a master painter—only no one else could see the mark. His arm slid around her waist from behind and yanked her back against him. Lil sucked in a breath as warm air rushed over her neck and his lips brushed the outer curve of her ear. She shivered. A delicate quake that shimmied from her head to her toes.

"You're not getting away from me this time, Lilli." He wrapped his other arm around her middle and spooned her body with his.

"Mac." Lillian straightened her spine, tried to put space between them, but Mac tightened his grip, keeping their bodies pressed together.

"Watch the game. Things are about to get interesting." His words, whispered against her ear, sent a shower of warmth down her back.

Heat radiated off him and soaked all the way through to her bones. She couldn't stop her muscles from softening, couldn't prevent herself from melting into his embrace. Lil focused on the game in front of her but she didn't really see it. The room and people filling it faded out as her mind zeroed in on the pounding of Mac's heart as it beat a steady tattoo along her back. Each thump hammered home the knowledge that this man could ask for anything and she'd be powerless to refuse.

He took a step backwards, tugging her with him as he moved to the rear of the crowded room. They could still see the game, but Lil no longer paid attention. How could she when Mac's fingers were stroking her flesh through the thin material of her dress? The silky cloth sliding over her skin added to his sensual caress and fired starbursts of sensation through every nerve ending. His hand slid higher until his fingers brushed the underside of her breast. Her nipples pebbled and goose bumps sprang up like waves on sand. The tiny mounds of awareness rippled back and forth as Lil's body flushed with arousal.

Mac dipped his other hand lower. He palmed her hip before inching his way to the hem of her little black dress and slipping questing fingers up the back of her thigh. Lil's knees shook as he teased her with a barely there touch. She sank her teeth into her bottom lip to stifle the moan bubbling in her throat. He skimmed his fingertips over the seam between her arse and leg, the stroke light, her reaction anything but. Her hips bucked, drove her buttocks into the cradle of his pelvis and the hard ridge of his cock pressed between her cheeks, the material of their clothes not hiding the evidence of his desire.

Lillian whimpered when Mac thrust forward. He cupped her breast and tweaked her nipple, the hard pinch turning the nub into a throbbing point of need. The hand beneath her skirt pushed higher, his fingertips probing the crease between her legs from behind. Moisture soaked her underwear, the thin strip of her thong no barrier to the flood of arousal he was drawing from her core. Mac nuzzled the side of her neck, his lips and tongue dancing on the sensitive area below her ear.

His grip on her breast tightened and the hand beneath her dress grew more daring. With ease, Mac pulled aside her underwear and strummed the slick folds of her pussy. Lil gasped as her body jolted with the electric touch. He probed deeper and she shifted her feet to part her legs. Her hands came up to grip his forearm and her elbow jabbed the man beside them. The sudden reminder of where they were—that they weren't alone—worked better than a bucket of cold water dumped over her head.

"Mac, stop." She dug her fingers into his arm and tried to pull away.

"Why? I know you like it." To prove his point, he swirled his fingertips through her wet slit.

Lillian clamped her legs together and angled her pelvis away, breaking the contact between his knowledgeable touch and her heated centre. "No." She pulled free only to find herself spun around and brought nose to nose with an angry Mac.

"Isn't this what you want? For me to touch you?"

"Yes. No." Lillian quickly took in the people around them, making sure no one was listening. "Not here. Someone will see."

Mac stared at her. "You parade around half naked for the whole world to see for a job, but you're worried about someone seeing us?"

"Of course I am."

He surveyed the people near them before bringing his gaze back to hers. His lips curled in the smile Lil referred to as his deal-maker smile, the one he got when he knew the next words out of his mouth would be the final blow in the argument, leaving him on the winning side. "You had me there for a second, but we all know Lillian McDermott loves nothing more than to be the centre of attention, so the fact the crowd is focused on your brother is your real problem, isn't it?"

"What?"

"You love the spotlight. I'd even go as far as saying you crave it. Why else would you flaunt yourself the way you do?"

She was dumbfounded. Did he honestly think she was the sum total of her model image? "That's how you see me?"

"It's hard to miss, Lilli. You spend your days in front of the camera. I think your image has well and truly been captured centre stage."

Her heart ached. How could he not know her? *Easy when you've never let anyone but Cam know the real you.* Lillian ignored the voice of reason in her head and took a step away from Mac. "You know, for a highly intelligent man you're rather stupid sometimes, Mac. What you see on billboards, in magazines and wherever else my picture appears is Lillian McDermott the model. She's an image, a two-dimensional figure without substance. It's a part I play, but it isn't and never has been the *real* Lillian, and you of all people should know that."

Tears burned her eyes, but she refused to let them fall. Lillian sucked in a breath and used the sudden movement of the crowd to make her escape. She lowered her gaze so as not to make eye contact with anyone and pushed her way from the room. A gasp emitted from the group behind her but she didn't turn to see what had happened in the game. She didn't care. The only thing on her mind was getting away from Mac and finding somewhere quiet to regroup. The house pulsed around her, the party in full swing, every room filled with the crush of bodies and loud music.

She turned towards the rear of the house, the laundry room off the kitchen her destination. Lil wasn't sure what upset her more, the fact she'd been so successful in portraying a superficial image, or that Mac hadn't been able to see through her disguise. Either way, the pain in her heart threatened to bring her undone. Her eyes and nose stung with unshed tears, and the sob building in her chest pressed against her rib cage, strangling her breath.

Lil stumbled through the kitchen and bumped into a waiter. The empty tray in his hands crashed to the floor, but she couldn't stop. If she didn't make it to the laundry room in the next few seconds, she'd lose it completely. Her fingers curled around the door handle, the metal cool beneath her skin as she turned the knob and pushed inside.

"Damn you, Mackenzie Harris."

Leaning back against the closed door, Lillian did something she'd done a hundred times before. She cried over Mac.

MAC STARED at the back of Lilli's head as she ran from the room. From him. What the hell just happened? She'd been into what he was doing, there couldn't be any doubt when the scent of her coated his fingers, but where it went wrong remained a mystery. He deserved more than the mini-lecture she'd given him. In his gut, he knew she wasn't anything like what he'd said. Known the words were designed to hurt her as he'd said them. So why had he?

For the past few months he'd gone nearly insane trying to reach her. Each time he'd gotten close she'd slipped from his grasp. And she was still eluding him. At least now Mac could say he'd actually spoken to her, touched her. But it wasn't enough. He needed to get her alone so they could talk. Really talk. He wanted to make up for his stupid comments and heaven knows there'd been plenty of them over the last year. He'd screwed up on multiple occasions, sabotaged any connection they may make with his own idiocy.

He could see some grovelling in his future. Mac had decided years ago that she was off-limits, but the explosive chemistry between them changed all that. Lachlan could be an issue, but Mac would worry about his best friend later. First, he needed to find Lilli and apologise for being a dumb-arse. Before he could take a step, the room erupted in a roar of cheers and stamping feet. The people in front of him moved and he could no longer see what was happening on the Twister mat.

"Everyone out." Lachlan's steely voice brokered no argument.

Instant silence descended and then as one the mass of bodies moved towards the door. When Lachlan McDermott gave an order, you followed and everyone in the room knew it. Mac was swept up in the avalanche of retreating partygoers, and he only just managed to stop from being bowled over in the rush. Pausing at the door, Mac stopped to make sure the stragglers left.

"Come on, out we go," he said.

Mac didn't quite catch what the weather guy said, but he wasn't all that pleased with the way the man kept looking back at Lachlan and Kole.

"Hey, you might want to mind your own business if you want to work in the industry ever again," he warned. Mac turned to leave with the last of the crowd. Intent on getting out without injury and looking for Lilli, he was pulled up short when Lachlan spoke again.

"Mac?"

"Lachlan?" He had no clue what his friend could want.

"Lock it."

Mac paused. Lock the door? Uh-oh, this didn't bode well for one reclusive former supermodel, but he had other things to worry about besides what Lachlan would do. He waited until the last person cleared the doorway ahead of him before flicking the lock and closing the door behind him. For a moment, he stared at the closed door, wondered if maybe that was the way to get Lilli to stay put, lock them in a room together and not let her out until he'd had his say and she'd forgiven him.

He had to find her first. No easy task with the number of people in his house. And he was one hundred percent positive she'd be going out of her way to avoid him. More than she already had tonight and the past seven months. With a sigh, he turned towards the foyer but couldn't see her anywhere. He glanced over his shoulder but there was no sign of her. There was no getting around it, he'd have to comb the house from top to bottom and back again until he found her. It would be like looking for a needle in a haystack.

3

MAC HAD SEARCHED every room in the house twice and was on his third circuit when he finally spotted Lillian. His jaw clenched. Two brawny guys had her sandwiched between them, their sides pressed against hers. It was totally unnecessary as far as he was concerned as there was ample room around the table. They leaned towards her, crowding into her personal space as she laughed at something one of them said. He wanted to walk over, shove them both aside and pull her out of her seat, away from the game.

Spin the bottle.

His hands fisted, fingers curled into his palm until the sting of his nails gave him a focal point other than the murderous thoughts he currently had. Mac kept his distance. He didn't want to tip Lilli off to his presence yet. Eight players circled the table, two of whom were at present engaged in a game of tonsil hockey. The bottle sat in a round container that had dividing lines dissecting the base in equal eighths. A pile of cards were passed from one of the tonsil-hockey participants to the guy on

Lilli's left. Mr. Muscles flipped over the top card and grinned. With a twist of his wrist, he sent the bottle spinning.

Everyone quietened down as the guy read out the card in his hand. "Round and round the bottle goes, where it stops nobody knows. When your turn is done it's time for fun. Before it ends, kiss arse or you won't be friends."

What the fuck? Mac remembered spin the bottle as a simple spin-and-kiss game, this adult adaptation didn't remotely resemble anything in his memory. He stood straighter and angled himself for a better view of that spinning glass vial. Each rotation knotted his gut muscles tighter. The thought of it coming to a halt with the neck pointing in Lilli's direction had him grinding his teeth. There was no way he would let that creep get his mouth anywhere near her rear end.

A gust of air burst from his lungs as the bottle slowed and finally came to a stop facing away from Lilli. The blonde woman across the table pushed back her chair and stood. With a grin that appeared alcohol assisted, she jumped up on the seat and thrust her miniskirt-covered arse out.

"Come on, Daryl, pucker up." Giggling, she wobbled on the chair but gained her balance by grabbing the shoulders of the guy next to her.

"Careful, Jessica," her rescuer said.

Mac was pretty sure it was Australia's notoriously famous womanizing cricket star stopping Jessica from taking a tumble. He wasn't at all surprised to see the athlete leaning over to get a good look up the woman's super-short skirt, or that he managed to cop a feel of her boobs while holding her steady.

Daryl made it around the table in an instant and wasted no time with the arse kissing. Mac's mouth dropped open when Daryl grabbed the hem of Jessica's skirt and pushed it up to reveal bare skin. Shocked to find himself unable to turn away, he watched as Daryl did far more than kiss arse. Jesus, the guy buried his face in the woman's crotch and proceeded to eat her out with everyone looking on. Neither of them seemed to recall where they were as they became engrossed in their foreplay. And that's what it was. Mac had watched plenty of porn in his life, even been to a sex show or two, but this wasn't about the audience, it was about the participants. He'd never been so turned on and disgusted at the same time in his life.

Mac jerked his gaze away from the carnal display and focused on Lilli. She looked everywhere but at the couple across the table. Somehow the fact she wasn't watching like the rest of the partygoers unfurled a few of the ribbons of tension in his gut. Cheers and whistles filled the air, the roar of approval competing with the music pounding through the speakers placed in each corner of the room. In his peripheral vision, Mac saw the couple break apart and Daryl help the woman retake her seat before coming back to reclaim the one next to Lilli. Mac was pleased to see Lilli shift her chair away as the guy sat beside her.

Damn. Lilli was up next.

She pulled a card from the deck and turned it over. The men on either side of her leaned closer and Mac's chest rumbled with a growl. He wanted to rip their heads off and shove them up their arses. Wanted to unleash this irrational urge for violence on the two hapless men daring to be near his woman. *Shit. His woman?* When the fuck had she become his? Mac took a deep breath and drew on some of his legendary lawyer control. Acting like a Neanderthal wouldn't impress Lillian or help win her forgiveness. Then again, dragging her off by the hair would certainly make it clear to all he'd staked a claim.

Was he staking a claim? Or was he pissed off she'd rejected him. Again. He knew he wanted her, had for years, but he'd spent so long stamping on the feelings she evoked he couldn't be sure this wasn't just some macho attempt to salvage his ego—to save face. He'd like to think he was above that kind of behaviour. It didn't matter. Mackenzie Harris never lost a battle. Whether it be in the courtroom, boardroom or bedroom, he was king of his world and Lillian McDermott would soon know that what Mac wanted, Mac got.

LILLIAN FINGERED the card in her hand and thought about her options. She could pull out of the game before spinning the bottle or she could spin and wait to see who her partner would be before she chickened out. Her gaze flicked back to the words printed in bold red ink on the glossy white background. After the last spin-card, she'd hoped for something less adventurous. A simple kiss would have been her preferred choice. Instead, Lil was stuck with the one in her hand, and she either took one shot now or spun the bottle and, depending on the targeted player, downed four shots as her penalty.

The men on either side of her jostled closer, each trying to get a look at what was written on her card. But she wasn't about to give anything away before making her decision, so she tucked it close to her chest. If she forfeited before the spin, her card got shuffled back into the deck without anyone ever knowing what her challenge had been. She just needed to decide if she wanted everyone to know what could make Lillian McDermott yellow-bellied. Another glance at her card, a quick scan of the rhyme and Lil made up her mind.

Her fingers trembled as she leaned over and grabbed hold of the bottle. Taking a deep breath, she tightened her grip and with a turn of her wrist, sent the glass spinning. Lil sat back and raised the card to eye level, effectively blocking her view of the rotating cylinder.

"Round and round the bottle goes, where it stops nobody knows. There is no work in a game of chance, but your partner has earned themselves a lap dance."

All the men around the table sat up straight, their gaze's glued to the spinning bottle as it slowed. Even the women seemed eager for the turn to end. Lil held her breath, mentally ticking off the table's occupants one by one, deciding who she might or might not be willing to give a lap dance. The chair next to her jerked to the side, bumping into hers, but Lillian had her full attention on that rapidly slowing bottle and ignored the disruption. She forced herself to suck in a long drawn-out breath through her mouth as each turn brought her closer to her final decision. A recognizable scent tickled her memories but she was too engrossed in the game to think of its origin.

Next to her, Daryl's chair scrapped forward on the floor and he leaned sideways until his thigh brushed hers, the soft well-washed denim warm against her bare skin. Denim? Wasn't he wearing board shorts? She glanced down quickly and noted the stone-washed fabric covering the leg next to hers before moving her gaze back to the spinning bottle. Surely Daryl hadn't left the table mid spin? Lil was on the verge of turning her head to see who'd joined the game when an arm shot out. A big hand wrapped around the glass bottle and stopped it with the neck in the section adjacent to hers. Lillian stared at the arm. The long, lean muscles, the sprinkling of golden hair and the very expensive, very familiar gold watch spanning the wrist.

Mackenzie.

Lillian squeezed her eyes shut, opened them and blinked several times before she gave up the hope she was seeing things. She'd know that watch anywhere. She remembered the hours spent searching for the right one. It had been the one and only time she'd allowed her true feels for Mac to show in a gift.

Every other present she'd given him had fallen into the friend-of-my-brother category. But that watch, with its yellow-and-white-gold band, the diamond-studded face and Swiss precision mechanics had stepped over the friend line and then some. That timepiece was something a woman bought for the man she loved.

And she had loved him—*did* love him. First with the bloom of a young girl's crush and newly discovered hormones. And then with the deeper emotions that came with maturity and knowledge. She tried too many times to count to aim her affections at other boys, other men, but none of them affected her the way Mac did. Even when she wanted to strangle him, she wanted to kiss him while her hands tightened around his neck. Lillian swallowed over the lump in her throat and turned her head, brought her gaze up to meet his.

Eyes the colour of a clear summer sky stared back. Their shade of blue was almost too pretty for a male, but there was nothing soft about the emotions churning in their depths. Desire, need and anger all mixed together in a maelstrom of conflicted sentiment. She knew that look, had seen it numerous times in the past. He wanted her, but he didn't want to, and that was the rub. For Lil that denial translated as a rejection of her, and she couldn't live with the ache in her heart anymore. As much as it would hurt, she needed to cut her loses and run.

"Pass the tequila." She curled her trembling fingers around her shot glass.

"No." Mac grabbed her wrist and stood. "You'll give me what I earned."

Lillian sucked in a breath, tried to get her mind to find a plausible excuse to deny him. "You cheated."

He pulled her to her feet and brought them eye to eye. "My house, my rules."

"But...but, you can't do that." She stumbled in her five-inch heels as he tugged her away from the table.

"Hey, man, you can't just barge in and steal a player," the international cricket player sitting opposite her protested.

Mac eyed the guy across the table. "Can. Did." He turned and towed her behind him as he stalked away from the game.

"Mac, you can't do this." She twisted her arm in a futile attempt to free herself, but his grip didn't loosen. "Mac."

"Not yet, Lilli." The look he shot her over his shoulder had her teeth sinking into her lip.

She could only imagine the expression on his face as people moved out of his way. Like the Red Sea, they parted without a word. Some of the women gazed at her with envious eyes and Lillian almost laughed. Under normal circumstances she's be thrilled to be with Mac, but right now wasn't normal. He was angry. Angrier than she'd ever seen him. His muscles strained with tension and the raw vibrations came off him in waves. Any fool in Mac's way would see them. They'd left the room and were heading for the stairs.

"At least tell me where we're going."

"My room."

Uh-oh. Lillian's stomach dropped to her toes, her heart sped up and beat against her ribs as though it were knocking to get out. They'd almost reached the top of the stairs and Lil knew there'd be no escape if he managed to get them any closer to his room. "Mac, stop. You're causing a scene."

He threw his head back and laughed, the sound humourless and scornful, but his stride didn't falter. He continued up the last few steps and pulled her behind him. When they were both on the upstairs landing, he spun her around and pinned her to the wall. "I'm making a scene? You've got half-naked celebrities sucking face and kissing arse and I'm the one creating a scene? I don't think so, Lilli. You'll have to do better than that to get away from me this time."

Mac held his gaze steady on hers. The blue orbs were charged with electricity that arced between them and sent a shiver down her spine. His stare dared her to contradict him, but she couldn't. He was right. No one took any notice of them, well, no more than they did the rest of the people in the house. No words came to mind, and before they could he lowered his mouth to hers.

She expected a harsh, angry kiss, but his lips were soft on hers. Their warm breath mingled as he brushed his tongue along the curve of her mouth. Mac watched her as he took the kiss deeper, his eyes taking in far more than she was ready to give. She lowered her eyelids as though they could shield her from him, but it was too late. A whimper of surrender and need slipped from her throat and he interpreted the small sound as permission to plunder. He drove his tongue between her lips, pushing past her teeth to stroke the roof of her mouth before teasing her tongue out to tangle with his. The second she gave in and did some demanding of her own, he groaned and pressed his body to hers.

The hard wall at her back and Mac's hard muscles along her front made her blood heat and her pulse pound. Her hips bucked against him and the solid length of an impressive erection prodding her thigh drew a moan from deep in her chest. He thrust into her, ground his cock on her leg and mimicked the rhythm with his tongue in her mouth. Lil's pussy clenched, flooded with heat and moisture as her knees shook.

"Hey, man, can I have some of that when you're done?"

They broke apart, each of them breathing hard as they sucked in vital oxygen. Lil wanted to lean forward, press her mouth to his once more and continue their mind-numbing kiss, but Mac's mouth turned down in a scowl and his brows dipped in the middle as his eyes narrowed. As she watched, the lust swirling in his eyes turned to anger. She sighed. There would be no more kisses.

With a growl aimed at the well-known football player standing beside them, Mac grabbed her hand and, threading his fingers through hers, started down the hall. Before she could protest or gain her senses and stop him, Lillian found herself inside his room with the door shut and locked behind them.

MAC LOCKED the door and tugged Lillian over to the bed. Noise from the party still thumped through the walls, but at least he could hear himself think in here. He stopped at the foot of his bed and was slammed with a bolt of lust. The urge to push Lilli onto the mattress and follow her down gripped him. In seconds, they could be naked and rolling across the sheets. Bad idea. It wouldn't solve anything if they had sex now.

He let go of her hand and stalked over to the window. The yard below was lit up like a Christmas tree. Barely clothed people swayed to the music blasting from every room of the house. His fingers curled around the window frame and his knuckles ached as he squeezed his hands tighter and tighter. Mac would love nothing more than to put a fist through the wall, but he'd never been one to give in to violence. Never really felt the need to inflict damage pump through his veins like it did this evening. Twice now Lil had reduced him to a base animal he had no experience with.

"Mac?"

Her breath fanned the hair on his neck. She'd stepped up behind him. He breathed deep, pulled her scent through his nose and into his lungs. The delicate fragrance that haunted his dreams, invaded his blood, flooded his mind and filled his cock with need that saturated his body. A burst of laughter echoed in the hallway on the other side of the closed door and brought his anger rushing back.

"Why, Lilli?" he asked.

"Why what?"

He turned around to look at her. "Why turn the house into a three-ring circus the first time you set foot back in the country in months?"

"I resent the implication that this party is out of control, Mac." She spun away and headed for the other side of the room.

"Isn't it? Were you even looking at what was going on down there?" He leaned his arse on the windowsill and crossed his arms. "Or is this the type of party you usually attend?"

"There's nothing wrong with the party. You're just pissed off I didn't ask your permission to hold it."

"Why wouldn't I be? It's not exactly what came to mind when I got your message. And I'm not the only one pissed off either. Lachlan is ready to spit nails."

"Lachlan should concern himself with his own life before he butts into mine, and so should you. I'm not a child, and if I want to throw a party for my friends, I will."

"Friends? You call those people downstairs friends?" Mac couldn't believe she thought of that shallow bunch of celebrities as friends. "I hate to break it to you, Lillian, but your group of so-called *friends* are here for one reason and one reason only."

"Oh, and what might that be, Mackenzie?" One eyebrow arched and she crossed her arms, stretching the skin-tight dress over her breasts and sending a spike of arousal through his balls.

"What you can give them." He pushed off the wall and walked towards her, hoping the movement would focus his brain on something other than his throbbing groin. "You don't think they actually want to spend time with you, do you?

They're here to be seen. To hopefully get their photo in the Sunday paper, or even better, be photographed with either of the McDermott siblings."

"That's a very shallow view of the world I live in, Mac. But then perhaps you have intimate knowledge of the attitude."

"What's that supposed to mean?" he spoke through clenched teeth. If she was implying he was one of those vultures who preyed on others for what they could give him, he'd strangle her. Or better yet, turn her over his knee and spank her arse.

"Let's face it, Mackenzie, you wouldn't be where you are today without tying yourself to Lachlan like you have all these years."

"Why you fucking little..." Mac moved before he thought. He had no clue of his intention when he grabbed her upper arms, but the second he touched her all thought fled except one. Tasting her.

"Mac?"

He dragged her against him and crushed her mouth beneath his, squashing any further protest. Filled with a volatile mix of frustration and arousal, the kiss was rough—hard. Lil remained rigid in his arms, but she didn't try to push him away. She let him take, and her lack of resistance dissolved any lingering anger he had.

Mac broke the kiss and stepped back. Lil wobbled a little before lowering herself to the floor as he sank to the bed behind him.

"I'm sorry." He stared at the woman before him. "I don't...I didn't mean..." Mac shook his head. He had no idea what he was trying to say, what he should say other than sorry.

Lilli sat in front of him. She'd bent her knees and rested her chin on top of them. Her beautiful baby blues looked at him with an understanding that obviously eluded him.

"Will it always be this way, Mac?"

Her question only added to his confusion. "What way?"

"Like a battle ground between us. It seems like we're always at odds with each other."

"All's fair in love and war." He tried to make a joke but it fell flat even to him.

Lilli laughed, the sound harsh and grating. "There's never been any love where you're concerned, only war."

"Maybe that's the problem."

"What is?"

"We've been too busy concentrating on the war part."

Lillian pushed to her feet and looked down at him with pity in her eyes. "I've never had that problem, Mackenzie."

"What's that supposed to mean?"

She turned away and strode to the door. "You're an intelligent man, you work it out."

The lock slid free with a click and Lilli left him sitting on the bed trying to piece together the conversation. Hell, the whole last few minutes. He'd never forced himself on anyone. Guilt and self-loathing assaulted him. She should have slapped him. He deserved more but that wasn't Lilli's style. No, physical retaliation wasn't her way. She'd use something far more devastating—more painful. Lilli would take away the one thing he couldn't live without. Her.

Mac got up and walked over to the window. The sounds of the party raged on and the yard below seemed fuller than before. He couldn't think straight with all this noise around him. He'd love nothing more than to jump in his car and go for a drive, but he couldn't even do that. There were at least four cars parked in front of the garage doors. Cars that belong to God knew who. With a sigh, Mac turned away and walked to the door. No point hiding out in his room, he may as well get a beer and find someone he wanted to talk to.

Lilli would be his first choice, but she'd be back to avoiding him after what he'd done. Besides, they could both do with some distance. He needed to work out what she'd meant with her parting words. Maybe then he could figure out what the hell was going on other than a serious case of lust. Even now, he had a hard-on thinking about her. Her taste lingered on his tongue and he licked his lips in search of more. His cock throbbed and his sac constricted, pulling his balls up. Jesus. What kind of arsehole kissed a woman in anger and got off on it? Mac wouldn't blame her if she never let him touch her again.

LILLIAN SPLASHED another handful of cold water on her face. She'd need to repair her makeup before returning to the party but that was the least of her worries right now. The confrontation with Mac had been eye-opening. He had no idea how she felt. All this time she'd thought he knew, thought he'd pushed her away and fought with her to keep her at arm's length so he wouldn't hurt her, but it was himself he was fighting.

She wasn't sure how she'd missed it before. Mac not only didn't want to want her, but he was completely oblivious to the fact she wanted him in return. It never occurred to her that he'd be blinded by his own anger and fear he wouldn't see how she felt about him. Lillian was pretty sure Lachlan knew how she felt about his best friend, but he'd never said anything to her and she definitely hadn't thought to confide in him. Even Cameron didn't know.

Thinking of her friend reminded Lillian she needed to get back to the party and check on her. Lil didn't think her brother would intentionally hurt Cam, but he didn't know the woman or what she'd been through, and it was easy to picture him doing damage to her friend's psyche with his alpha-male persona. Not that Cam was delicate at all. She could definitely look after herself, but Lil would feel better knowing she hadn't brought either of them harm by arranging this meeting.

Lillian made quick work of patching up her makeup. Years of modelling had taught her quite a few tricks when it came to camouflaging the flaws nature dished out. Dark circles, blemishes and premature winkles were easily dealt with when you knew how. Satisfied she looked presentable, Lil left her bathroom and slipped back into the heels she'd discarded by her bedroom door when she'd sought the sanctuary of her private space.

The metre-by-metre poster board leaning on the far wall caught her eye and she walked over to admire Cam's work for the millionth time. Lillian had been in a simple gold dress that flowed over her curves like water and her body was arched to emulate the bottle in her hand. She'd had the shape of the perfume bottle designed to resemble a calla lily and she'd been very impressed with the results. Pleasure filled her when she thought about the upcoming launch. They'd managed to keep the whole Golden Lilli project a secret, from conception to fruition, this was one more part of her dream, and Lil couldn't wait for the ad campaign to go live.

She smiled as she moved across her room. She turned the handle and opened the door. The noise hit her square in the face. Music, laughter and the general sounds associated with people having a good time. Mac might be right, most of the partiers were no more than acquaintances, but that wouldn't stop her from putting on the party of the year. Tonight was a celebration of finally reaching her dream. Of course, no one but Cam and Cassie knew that. Still, it didn't matter. Tonight would be her last hurrah to a world she'd never felt at home in.

4

MAC COULDN'T FIND Lachlan anywhere. There was no sign of Kole either, but the library was open again and another rowdy game of Twister was well underway, so he could only assume his friend hadn't killed the woman who had starred in Lachlan's—and millions of other men's—teenage fantasies. He wandered the house with a beer in his hand for close to an hour. The party had revved up while he'd been upstairs with Lillian.

Lilli.

Her name whispered through his mind like a gentle breeze on a summer afternoon. It was a tantalising promise of relief but only succeeded in reminding him of how hot he was to begin with. As much as he wanted to deny his feelings for her, or put them down to pure lust, he couldn't. He'd known her since she was five. He knew her heart, her generous nature and the way she chose to see only the good in people. She never had a bad word to say about anyone, even those who did her wrong weren't treated badly, only subjected to what he liked to refer to as the Lillian McDermott dust off.

She always conducted herself with dignity and courtesy. Her faultless demeanour had been something he'd admired. Right up until she'd followed in her mother's footsteps out onto the catwalk. Maybe that was his problem. Her chosen career was so at odds with the girl he'd watched grow up, a contradiction to the woman she should have become. Then again, who was he to say he knew the real Lillian. She'd accused him of not knowing her earlier, and perhaps she was spot on, because he couldn't understand or mesh the two individuals who made up Lillian McDermott.

Before he could dwell on his thoughts further, a woman who looked familiar but he couldn't put a name to stepped next to him and offered another beer.

"I'd say you're ready for a new one. You've nursed that one for a while." She smiled.

Mac glanced at the shirt she wore, the bold script across her breasts marking her as part of the company running the show. He traded his half-empty warm one for the ice-cold bottle she held out. "Thanks."

Her gazed skimmed the room before coming back to his. "The party's going great, isn't it?"

"Humph." Mac bought the bottle to his lips and took a swig.

"Look, Mac, I get that you didn't agree to this party, but Lil deserves to enjoy this one night. She's worked her arse off for this. Can't you at least pretend to be happy for her?" Her voice took on an accusing edge.

"Ha. From what I can see, the company you work for has done all the work, all Lillian had to do was dress up and sashay out into the room." Mac couldn't help the snarl of disgust lacing his words.

"I'm not talking about setting tonight up, I'm referring to the last five years of working at a job she at times despised to achieve her ultimate dream." The woman whose name still escaped him turned his way and lowered her voice. "She's built Lilli Pond from the ground up without a handout from Daddy or big brother. The very least you can do is respect her for that, even if you don't agree with her choices."

"Lilli Pond?" Mac had no idea what this woman was talking about. And the fact that he couldn't remember her name when he knew he should just pissed him off more.

"Cassie!" A guy in a similar shirt to the brunette rushed over. "We need you in the kitchen. We're running out of scotch."

Cassie. Cassandra Moreland. Of course. Lillian's best friend from high school.

"I'll handle it, Dan." She turned back to Mac. "Let her say goodbye to the world she's never been comfortable in on her terms."

"Goodbye?" Where the hell was Lilli going? "What do you mean goodbye?"

Cassie's eyes widened. "Y-you didn't know?"

"Didn't know what?"

"That Lil quit modelling." Cassie glanced around them. "I shouldn't have said anything. I didn't know she hadn't told you. I have to go."

In the next breath, Mac was alone. Lilli's friend disappeared into the crowd with the skills of a highly trained security expert. He shook his head. What the fuck was Lilli Pond and when the hell had Lilli quit modelling? It was the first he'd heard of either, but he wasn't about to remain in the dark. Mac stood on the balls of his feet, stretching until he could see over the tallest of occupants in the room. There was no sign of Lilli. Well, he'd just have to do what he'd done earlier. Search the house from top to bottom until he found her. But in the meantime there was more than one way to find out what he wanted to know.

Mac pulled his phone from the front pocket of his jeans. For a second, he thought about ringing the head of McDermott Security to find out what Lucas Wilhelm knew about Lilli Pond, but only for a second. A much faster option was right at his fingertips. He swiped his thumb over the screen and tapped to open a search window. *Google is my friend.* Smiling, he typed in Lilli Pond.

It took no time for a multitude of links to come up. By the time he'd scanned through the sixth one he'd discovered two things. Lilli Pond was a hugely successful children's clothing label and the owner was extremely secretive. Not once did the name of the person behind the business appear in any of the articles or the company website. If Lilli was behind it, and Mac had a sinking feeling in his gut that she was, she'd kept her name out of the spotlight. Or more importantly, the McDermott name.

He glanced at his watch and decided it wasn't too late to find out a little bit more. He scrolled through his phonebook, found the number he was after and hit call. When Lucas answered, Mac wasted no time with pleasantries.

"Lucas. Get me everything you can on a company called Lilli Pond and what Lillian McDermott has to do with it."

"I can give you what information we have right now, sir."

"Well?" Mac stuck a finger in his ear and headed for the back deck, hoping to find the yard less noisy.

"Ms. McDermott has owned and operated the company for three years. This year the business made more than its overheads and she no longer has to supplement the bank accounts with her personal funds."

"That's it?"

"Pretty much, sir."

"Why is that all we have on it?" Mac couldn't believe McDermott Security had so little information. Either Lucas wasn't giving him everything or he hadn't done his job properly.

"Ms. McDermott came to me before she started the company. She gives me the barest of information every three months, with a full report every year, on the condition that I don't dig any further into the financials or make the information common knowledge," Lucas said.

"So you have no idea who works for her?" Mac asked.

"Oh, no, I have all that information. It's the same staff since she opened the doors. She allowed me to run full background checks on each of them, Mr. Harris."

"And you've never thought to mention this to me or Lachlan?"

"No, sir. She first came to me when you and Mr. McDermott were struggling with the fallout of the takeover from the senior McDermott. You can be assured that I would have come to either of you at any stage if I felt it was necessary. Excuse my frankness, sir, but Ms. McDermott has earned the right to my confidence. She's worked hard and never gone against anything I or a member of my team has asked her to do in all the years I've worked for McDermott Media Corp."

Mac wanted to argue, but he knew Lucas well, and he could hear the admiration and respect in the other man's voice. "Is there anything else I should know?"

"There is other information I could give, but unless I'm given the all clear from Ms. McDermott, or you give me information that leads me to believe you've found out something else, I won't be divulging it at this time."

"Damn. I'd like to demand you do, Lucas, but I respect you and your judgment, and if you tell me I shouldn't be worried, then I won't be." Mac stared out at the water that lapped onto the beach at the bottom of the backyard. "So, do I need to be worried, Lucas?"

"No, Mac."

Mac breathed a sigh of relief. He could trust Lucas Wilhelm with his life, so he certainly could accept the man's word about this. Plus, the fact he'd used Mac's first name spoke volumes. "You'd let me know if there was something to be concerned about?"

"In a heartbeat," Lucas assured him.

"Don't go to bed early tonight. I may need you later if this shindig Lillian has put on gets out of hand."

"I already have two men inside, sir."

Mac laughed. "Why am I not surprised? Guest or worker?"

"Worker." Mac could hear the smile in the other man's voice. "And don't bother looking, they're new on the payroll and employed just for this sort of occasion. No one knows them, including Mr. McDermott."

"Does Lilli know you have men staking the place out?" Mac asked with a smile.

The sound that blasted his eardrum could only be described as a snort.

"I'm still alive, aren't I?" Lucas replied through laughter.

Mac glanced over his shoulder and into the house. "Well, I'm not going to be the one to tell her they're here."

"If you call me and a team in, they'll remain catering staff. I don't want these men's identities compromised at all." Lucas's voice was stern and Mac could picture the man puffing up his chest as he gave the subtle order.

"No issue on my end, Lucas. I'll let you know if you're needed."

"No problem."

Silence met Mac's ear and he realised Lucas had hung up. Chuckling, he dropped his hand and slid the phone into his pocket. For long moments, Mac stood facing the sea. He thought about what he'd learned in the last few minutes and cursed himself for a fool. There were no excuses for his behaviour since Lilli had become a model. He'd treated her with contempt based on what her mother had been like. What kind of man does that? Especially to the woman he loves.

Mac sucked in a breath—his body going rigid. He loved her? His breath whooshed out. Well, of course he did. She was the little sister he never had. Except the way he felt had nothing to do with sisterly love. Arousal buzzed in his veins whenever he thought about her, never mind when he was near her. The sensations she provoked fried his brain and filled his cock with urgent need. A need so deep it singed his marrow and drove him near to madness. Could he have used her profession to keep her at arm's length?

He lowered his head and closed his eyes. He'd been a bastard on so many occasions. Accusing her of things because of what? Her choice of career? Fear? His lack of control whenever she was near? God, he'd been an arse and never once had she called him on it. All the time she was building a business, establishing a name for herself without using her actual name, he'd been scornful, disapproving, sanctimonious in his attitude towards her. And she'd let him get away with it. If he were Lilli, he'd never speak to him again.

Damn, he had some serious apologising to do. It shamed him to think of how badly he'd treated her. For all his accusations of her superficial lifestyle, he'd been the shallow one. Only seeing the one side of her, the one splashed all over the world, barely clothed, in sexy poses, tempting the male of the species to lust after her. That's the way he'd seen her modelling. He'd done what every other male on the planet had done. Looked at those glossy prints and thought he could see into her soul. Except he'd already seen Lilli's soul. He'd watched it blossom from child to teenager to woman and he'd ignored it and superimposed the image of her mother on top.

He was a fool. The biggest kind. The kind that cuts their nose off in spite of their face. But no more. From now on he wouldn't fight what he felt, wouldn't assume anything about her. Wouldn't let the guilt of falling for his best friend's sister get in the way either. It might feel like a betrayal of every best-mate code ever thought, uttered or written, but he couldn't deny what was in his heart.

Lilli. Now that Mac had opened his eyes he was determined to fix things between them. Only one problem stood in his way. Right now he was probably the last person she wanted to see. Good thing he had a thick skin and over the years of tough business negotiations had learned to hold on until he got what he wanted. Shame he couldn't have figured out sooner that what he wanted most was right in front of him all along.

LILLIAN'S FEET HURT. Her five-inch heels might be drop-dead sexy, but they were also torture devices designed to make her toes drop off. She headed into the kitchen for a much needed breather. While the party was a huge success and she should be thrilled, she wasn't. This wasn't how she pictured it. There was only numbness where euphoria should have been. She'd like to blame Mac. Why not? He'd been a source of misery for most of her life, so why couldn't he shoulder the blame for this too?

She slipped out of her shoes and sighed. Curling and uncurling her toes on the cool tiles brought some relief, but it was only temporary. She'd have to slide those damn sandals back on again in a moment and continue to smile while her blood refused to circulate. First thing next week, she was getting a pedicure. The deluxe version. Lil arched her back, stretched muscles sore from walking in heels for hours when in recent months she'd either been barefoot or wearing flip-flops. Maybe she'd spring for a full body massage.

Her feet protested as she shoved her abused toes into the strappy Jimmy Choo's. She may have been given the ultra-sexy stilettos after featuring in a shoot for the famous designer, but right now Lil couldn't think of one good reason why anyone would pay over five hundred dollars for some skinny strips of leather and heels that were thinner than ice picks. How she managed not to break her neck was a testament to her exceptional balance and determination to remain upright.

Shoes firmly in place, Lil turned to head back into the throng of partygoers when Aaron Watson entered the kitchen. He stumbled towards her and instinct, not any lingering feelings of affection for the man, had her reaching out to support him. His breath reeked of gin and Lil wasn't at all surprised by his inebriated state. Aaron had a weakness for alcohol. At least that's the way his doting parents referred to it. As far as Lil was concerned, the man was an alcoholic and needed a ten-step program. But who was she to argue in the man's favour. He'd lost his last friend credit when she'd been informed he'd leaked the photos of her sunbaking topless last year.

Aaron flung his arms around her neck and spoke against her cheek. "Is lofe ou."

Lil was fairly certain he didn't know the true meaning of the word love but figured in his small world what he felt for her was real. Not that she had ever returned his feelings. He'd never been more than an acquaintance in her youth, just two kids from families with money, but once she'd started modelling and socialising in a different circle he'd become a trusted friend. Of course, that was before the booby shots. She cringed. They weren't even flattering pictures.

"Come on, Aaron, let's find somewhere for you to lie down before you fall down. And take me with you." She manoeuvred his dead weight towards the laundry. There was plenty of floor space in there and no foot traffic—perfect for keeping his drunken arse out of sight too.

"Lie wiff me." He wasn't just slurring his words, he was sloshing them.

She tried to ignore the drool now covering her face, but between that and his clumsy attempts to land his mouth on hers, Lil was close to dropping him where they stood. Serve him right if the wait staff walked over him. They'd made it to the doorway and Lil reached out to open the door, but Aaron shifted in her grasp, making a valiant effort to grope her breasts, and they lost balance as she dodged his clammy grip. The door handle turned in her hand and they both went down as it opened. Hard.

A renting sound filled the air as her dress split at the seam. Lillian cursed. The dress was one of her favourites. Aaron would be compensating her for it as soon as he was sober. Right now though, she had to worry about getting him off her. She'd taken the brunt of the fall, her shoulder and side connecting with the ceramic tiles with a bone-bruising thump before Aaron's dead weight landed on her. It was hard to believe the red-faced drunk on top of her was one of Australia's favourite television hosts. Lillian pushed against his chest and attempted to shove him off. He didn't budge. All she got for her trouble was agony.

Her side throbbed and her left arm shook, a pain shooting up into her shoulder when she tried to put some strength behind her push. Aaron lay still, a dead weight flattening her breasts and squeezing the breath from her lungs. She wiggled around to shift him to the side and a glimpse of his face told her why getting him off proved so hard. He'd passed out, either from the alcohol he'd consumed or a bump to the head. Lil assumed it was the alcohol since she'd broken his fall, and the only place his skull had come in contact with was her nicely padded chest.

Lil turned her head to see if anyone had come over, but the laundry door was tucked around a section of wall and they'd landed inside the utility room. So unless somebody saw them fall, no one could see them from the kitchen area. She took another stab at shoving Aaron off, but he'd fallen in such a way that his body pinned down her non-injured shoulder and draped across her diagonally, his thick middle resting on her sore hip. No matter which way she moved, her left side pounded with sharp stabs of pain. Sucking in as deep a breath as she could, she gave it one more go. Lil's eyes stung with tears as fire shot from wrist to shoulder and her arm gave out.

She sank her teeth into her lip to stifle the agonised cry from leaving her throat. Gasping for air, she struggled to breathe through the painful waves. Eventually, they eased off until there was no more than a dull ache beating at her side. Resigned to the fact she wouldn't be able to move Aaron on her own, Lil gave in and opened her mouth to yell for help. But Aaron's weight disappeared before she made a sound. Her eyes fluttered closed as her lungs finally filled to the brim with oxygen.

"Lilli?"

Lil opened her eyes to see Mac's face swimming above her.

"Are you all right?"

She was vaguely aware of his hands running all over her.

"Talk to me!"

Her lips curled in a small smile. Mac cared.

"Dammit. Don't just lie there grinning. Answer me!"

"Okay." She licked her dry lips, swallowed to coat her parched throat. "I'm okay."

"You don't look okay." Mac's hand slid up her side. "Fucking Christ! Your dress is torn. What the hell did he do to you?"

Lil tried to sit, only to have Mac press on her sore shoulder to keep her down.

"Argh…" She clenched her jaw and closed her eyes against the dull pain. The only thing she could think was Aaron would be a dead man if anything was broken.

"Jesus." Mac ran his hands over her shoulder and down her arm, his fingers probing gently as he searched for serious injury. "There's no blood and I don't think you've broken anything but I can't be sure…"

"Jarred." Lil breathed through her words. "Hit the floor. Hard. Aaron fell. On me."

"What were you doing?"

Lillian could hear the strained anger in Mac's words and sort to reassure him. "He's drunk."

"I can smell that. Besides, I saw him staggering towards the kitchen and followed." He eased her off the floor and into his arms, his hands running down her spine. "I'd have gotten here quicker without all these people filling the place. Of course, the dickhead wouldn't be here then either."

She couldn't argue with that, but Aaron hadn't meant any harm and really, it was her own fault for trying to help the drunken idiot when he outweighed her by at least forty kilos. Although Lil was fairly sure Mac would blame him, and she didn't want to be around for that.

"Can you see my denim jacket?" she asked. Her head was tucked under Mac's chin and she felt his stubbled jaw catch in her hair as he looked around.

"Yeah, it's on a hanger over the tub."

"Help me up. I need to change out of this dress, but I can't walk through the house with the side split open." Now that her lungs were supplying oxygen to her brain and body, Lil realised her injuries weren't that bad. Jarred and winded was as severe as it got.

"You're not walking." Mac stood and scooped her into his arms. "I'll carry you to your room."

"No. Put me down." Lil squirmed against him. "I don't want to draw attention to myself or the situation, and being carted around the house by you will guarantee phones will be pulled out and pictures will hit Twitter and Facebook within seconds. Now. Put. Me. Down."

"Lillian."

"Mackenzie."

They stared at each other, neither willing to give an inch. It was Aaron's moan that broke their deadlock. Lil and Mac turned to look at the grumbling man—Mac with a snarl of disgust and Lil with a heavy ball of disappointment and sadness in her stomach. She had no illusions though. Aaron was one of many in her life who were only after what they could get from being Lillian McDermott's friend. But that was her old life. The one she would walk away from without a backward glance after tonight.

"Please put me down, Mac."

Mac let her legs drop, but he held on to her when her feet touched the floor. With his arm around her back, he ushered her deeper into the room. He steadied her against the counter before reaching to retrieve her jacket.

"Here. Can you put this on by yourself?"

"Yeah." Lil took the still-damp denim from his outstretched hand. She'd only need to make it up to her room, so thankfully the clammy fabric wouldn't be on for long.

Mac walked back to where Aaron lay muttering. He wrapped his hands around the other man's wrists and pulled.

"What are you doing?" Lil slid one arm into her jacket and cringed at the clingy sensation.

"Moving him out of the doorway so we can shut the door." Mac dragged a now spluttering Aaron across the floor.

"Why would we shut it?" Her other arm disappeared into the sleeve and she noticed the pain had almost gone. Lil reached for the zip.

"So he doesn't go out there and cause more havoc. Or come looking for you again." Mac glanced at her. "Are you going to tell me what happened?"

Lil closed the zipper halfway. She shivered. Her dress was no barrier to the moisture the material still held. "Not now. I need to get out of this dress."

"Come on then." Mac stepped forward with his hand out. "Stay close and I'll get you through the crowd without stopping."

She hesitated. It would probably be simpler if she ducked upstairs on her own.

"Don't even think of saying no, Lilli."

"But..."

Mac's gaze told her there'd be no arguing with him.

With a sigh, she placed her hand in his and allowed him to lead her from the room. He guided her through the door first and shut it behind them. She would have protested, but he shook his head and nudged her forward. As they passed through the kitchen, he tugged her closer to his side, let go of her hand and slipped his arm around her shoulder.

Lil marvelled at how swiftly Mac moved them through the house. She offered smiles to anyone who looked her way, but her companion obviously had a scowl on his face because everyone immediately turned away as they drew near. He marched them up the stairs, and by the time they reached the top she was out of breath.

"Slow down, Mac. It's not a race."

"Just keep up or I'll pick you up," he growled through clenched teeth.

She wasn't sure where the anger had come from. Other than the snatch of it back in the laundry, Mac hadn't shown anything but concern. Lil had a feeling that was about to change. They arrived at her door and she stopped, ready to thank him.

"Don't even think about it, Lilli." Mac gripped the doorknob, his knuckles blanching white.

"I can take it from here. You don't need to come inside." The door opened in front of her and Mac placed his hand on her lower back and propelled her forward. She spun around, her toes pinching in her shoes but she couldn't stop him from following her and shutting the door behind them. "Mac?"

"Get changed."

"I will when you leave." Lil folded her arms over her chest. The damp jacket was uncomfortable but she ignored it.

"Now. And when you're done I want to hear exactly what happened down in the laundry." He walked over to her bed and sat. With a calmness that grated on her nerves, Mac swung his legs up and stretched out on the mattress, his back resting against the headboard.

Lil contemplated arguing to get her way, but the combination of her damaged dress, wet jacket and aching side convinced her she'd be better off doing as he wanted. Of course, she'd give him an abridged version of her encounter with Aaron and hope it would be enough to make him go away. Then she could take a moment to assess the bruising that was sure to be peppered down her left side.

Slipping out of her shoes, she stalked towards her walk-in-robe. Grumbling under her breath about pushy men and drunken idiots, Lil searched for another dress to wear. She shrugged out of her jacket and hung it up, pushing the clothes on either side away to make sure the damp fabric would have air flow. She'd have to remember to take it outside tomorrow and let the sun freshen it up. Lil picked a summer shift that flowed loosely over her body. Her little black dress might look hot, but it had a tendency to stick to her skin in the heat.

New dress in hand, she gripped the gapping side of the one she wore and headed for the bathroom. Lil didn't even spare Mac a glance. He might think he was in charge, but not for long. Once she'd replaced her torn dress, she'd be ready to face him again.

5

MAC WAITED for Lilli to come out of her bathroom. She'd been in there less than a minute, but that was sixty seconds too long as far as he was concerned. He wanted to know what that arsehole downstairs had done to her. *Needed* to know. The rage that had surged through him when he'd seen her pinned beneath Aaron Watson had nearly crippled him. When he'd pulled the man off her and smelled the liquor emanating from the Armani-clad jerk, Mac's gut had rolled. Numerous scenarios had flashed through his mind between the time he dumped Watson's celebrity arse on the floor and checked on Lilli.

At first he'd thought the worst, and he still wasn't convinced he shouldn't go down and beat the shit out of one of Australia's favourite TV faces. Mac smiled, the image of a busted-up Aaron hosting his game show bringing mild satisfaction. But the incident furthered his anger at Lilli for having this stupid party in the first place. If she'd just stuck with what he wanted—

The door across the room opened and Lilli stepped out.

The black dress had been replaced with a skin-coloured one. But unlike the previous dress, this one didn't coat her body like paint. This one flowed, skimming over her curves like hot fudge on ice cream. He licked his lips and shifted position so she wouldn't see the hard-on that had sprung to life the second she moved into sight. Damn, she was sex on legs. Long, smooth, tan legs left bare by her mid-thigh-length hem.

She wandered over to where she'd kicked off her fuck-me heels and bent to slip them on. Her hem inched higher, giving him a flash of the silky skin on her inner thighs. He knew how soft that area was. Knew how it slid beneath his fingertips with tantalizing ease. Mac swallowed, his throat going dry as he remembered having his hand on that supple flesh earlier. God, she was a distraction. He'd entered her room with the intention of finding out how her dress had been torn, not to think about stripping her out of it.

Giving himself a mental shake, he swung his legs over the side of the bed and sat forward, his elbows resting on his knees, Mac continued to watch her move. "Tell me what happened."

She jerked, just a small jolt before her body went perfectly still. He studied her closely, didn't want to miss any telltale twitch or tick that may indicate she wasn't being honest with him. Mac had no doubt she would try to slip a pair of rose-coloured glasses over the incident. She'd do everything she could to minimise what had happened. Her chest rose as she sucked in a breath and brought her gaze around to meet his.

"We were talking, but Aaron obviously has had too much to drink and he stumbled." Her eyes skittered away for a second but she pulled her shoulders back and met his gaze once more. "Honestly, it was my own fault for trying to stop him from falling."

Mac narrowed his eyes. She was lying. Angry at her for protecting that shallow prick, he jumped to his feet and stormed across the room. He brought his face within a breath of hers. "Bullshit!"

Her eyes went wide and he watched as fear, guilt and finally anger slashed across their sparkling depths.

"Don't lie to me," he growled.

"You're forgetting one thing, Mac. I don't owe you anything, lie or not. I don't have to explain myself to you." She punctuated her final word with a finger poke to his chest.

With her shoes on they were eye to eye, and the fire shooting from hers did some seriously weird shit to his equilibrium. He'd always liked a good battle. He wasn't a brilliant lawyer for nothing, and regardless of Lillian's earlier accusation, he hadn't gotten where he was by riding his best friend's coattails. He liked to fight and hated to lose. Blood rushed through his veins, the thrill of combat causing an effect he'd never dealt with in the courtroom or anywhere else for that matter. His pants grew snug over his throbbing erection. A grin pulled at the corner of his mouth, but Mac refused to let it form completely. Heaven forbid Lilli work out he was getting off on their clash of wills.

"Yes. You do." He wrapped his fingers around her nape. "And this is why."

Mac slammed his mouth on hers. His tongue immediately thrust out to force its way between her lips. This wasn't a kiss. It was a claim. He took advantage of her gasp and pushed his way inside. *Heat.* Slick molten pleasure waited in the dark and he plunge deeper. Lilli held her body stiff in his arms, and everything he had, everything he was, wanted her to yield. To hand herself over completely. Freely.

He gripped her neck tighter, his fingers digging in, bringing her closer. Mac's other hand curled around her waist, scrunched silky fabric in his fist. She moaned, and the soft sound vibrated across his tongue and slipped down his throat as he breathed it in—breathed *her* in. Want and need overtook him. He'd never get over the way she made him yearn with such intensity. No more than a look, a simple movement, and his body went up in flames, but touch her...touch her and he spontaneously combusted. From the hair on his head to the nails on his toes, Mac exploded in a raging inferno he had no hope of extinguishing without her.

"Lilli." Mac breathed her name against her mouth before nipping at her plump lower lip. He suckled at the fleshy curve then licked with the flat of his tongue.

She shivered. The tremor reverberated through his chest and set off a shudder of his own. He had to have her. Had to feel her beneath him. On top of him. Surrounding him. Inside him. Mac dove back into her mouth, searched out her tongue and sucked hard. This time, when Lilli moaned she sank into him. Her body moulding to his like hot wax. He'd never felt a surrender like it. With one move, she made him ten feet tall and brought him to his knees.

Lilli tore her mouth from his and gasped for breath. "Mac. Please."

"Please what?" He peppered kisses along her cheek to her ear. "Tell me what you want, Lilli. Anything. God, I'll give you anything."

"You," she sighed as he licked the delicate skin of her neck.

"Be sure, once we start I won't be able to stop." He breathed in her ear. "I've wanted too long, Lilli."

Her pelvis rocked, her hips bumping into his, and a cry of pain tore from her throat. She pulled away, but he had a good grip and she didn't get far.

"What? What the hell happened?" Mac leaned back to look at her.

She shook her head. "Nothing. It was nothing." But she couldn't hide the pain in her eyes.

"No. It wasn't nothing." He clenched his jaw, his back teeth grinding together. "Tell me."

Lilli's perfect white smile appeared strained before her gaze left his and she chewed on the corner of her lip. A move he knew well. She was deciding whether or not to lie.

"Don't. Not now." Mac couldn't help the plea that followed. "Please, Lilli."

Her eyes closed and she lowered her forehead to rest on his shoulder with a sigh. "I've got a few bruises from the fall, that's all."

He saw red. Aaron had marked her. Mac's blood boiled and his muscles tensed. But it was no longer arousal driving his reactions. He'd never been a physical fighter. Always relied on his wits and words to get the better of others, but tonight... Tonight he wanted to smash heads and beat his chest like a caveman. Right after he'd grabbed the woman in his arms by her hair and dragged her back to his cave. Wrapping his arms around her back, he snuggled her against his body and tried to regain his balance. Not an easy feat when he teetered between lust and rage.

"Show me." Mac pushed her to arm's length. "Take that dress off and let me see."

"No."

"You and I both know I can have that off you in a second." Mac didn't want to force the issue, but he would if she didn't agree.

"Mac—"

"Don't. I don't want excuses or a fight." He took a deep breath and struggled to find the words to express the way he felt. "I have to see. *Need* to see with my own eyes. If I don't, Lilli... God, if I don't, I'll go mad."

She stayed quiet, studying him with those all-seeing blue eyes. He thought she would continue to argue when she pulled out of his grasp but she surprised him. Crossing her arms over her stomach, she gripped the dress at her hips and slowly brought the material up her body. As each new inch of bare skin was revealed Mac's blood pressure shot up. When her see-through panties came into view, he thought he'd swallow his tongue.

But then the first mark appeared and his blood ran cold. A red blotch that grew darker towards the centre marred her outer thigh just below her hip. It reminded him of the mark left by a slap and he cursed Watson once more. His gaze was glued to the hem of her dress as she raised it higher, but he wasn't prepared for the bruise on her hipbone. Already shades of black and blue, the darker section along her jutting bone clearly showed the impact point. Mac ground his teeth, his nostrils flaring as he sucked in a breath.

"Fuck." He reached out and brushed a fingertip over the bruise.

Lilli stilled, her thigh muscles quivering as he stepped closer and traced the outer edge of the ugly mark. He brought his gaze up to meet hers and flattened his hand over the curve of her hipbone, making sure to use the barest pressure.

"The rest." Mac tipped his chin to indicate the dress.

She pulled the dress all the way off. Dropping it to the floor at her feet, she stood before him in a matching bra and panties set. The strapless bra proved to be as see-through as the panties, and Mac fought against his baser urges to toss her on the bed and sink his cock between her legs. He tried to keep the emotions swirling inside him hidden by dropping his gaze to her side. Raising his hand, he twirled his finger in the air to prompt her to turn around. There was no way he could manage a verbal direction.

Lilli followed his unspoken request and Mac sucked in another deep breath as his gaze met the rest of her injuries. He could see the red marks along with more bruises already form-ing. They lined her left side in sections. It was obvious to him she'd come down heaviest on her hip but couldn't work out how when the rest of the damage was more to her side and back, plus she'd been pinned to the floor on her back.

"Tell me how you fell again?"

"Aaron lost his balance and I couldn't hold his drunken dead weight so we went down." She shrugged. "Why do you keep asking?"

"Because all your injuries make sense except this one." Mac ran his fingers lightly over her hipbone.

She glanced down, her forehead creasing as she stared at his fingers as they traced the ugly bruise.

"These marks." Mac brushed his fingertips over the ones along her side. "They're all consistent with you hitting the floor with your left side at a bit of an angle. But not this one." Mac cupped her hip in his palm.

"Oh." She chewed the corner of her mouth. "I think our bodies clashed in the fall. He had on that stupid belt buckle he always wears too. That must have connected with my hip."

Mac took a deep breath and asked the question he wasn't sure he wanted the answer for. "Did he hurt you any other way?"

Lilli stared at him, confusion swirling in her eyes. She shook her head twice before her eyes went wide with compre-hension. "Oh, God, no. No, he didn't hurt me Mac."

Breathing a sigh of relief, he said, "We should put a cold compress on these bruises."

"No, it's okay. I'll be fine."

"You know, I can't decide if I want to hold you close and kiss all those spots better or go downstairs and break Watson's nose." Mac stepped closer. "What do you want me to do, Lilli? It's your choice."

She licked her lips and Mac had to stifle a groan. He leaned forward, brushed her lips with his and caught her sigh on his tongue when she opened for him. Mac kept the kiss gentle. With lush strokes and slow caresses, he coaxed her into joining him. Nothing touched but their mouths and his hand palming her hip. Lilli moved into him. Her body pressed flush to his and he knew he no longer needed an answer to what he should do, but he wanted one all the same.

He broke their mouths apart and rested his forehead to hers. "What do you want me to do, Lilli?"

Her breath came fast and shallow, their simple kiss affecting her as much as it had him. A shiver rippled through her and her breasts lifted, her nipples pointy little beads beneath their lace covering. "Kiss me better."

It was all the invitation he needed.

Mac scooped her into his arms and carried her to the bed. He placed her on the mattress, nudged her over to the middle and crawled on beside her. On his knees, he leaned over and skimmed his fingertips up and down her arms before trailing them over her shoulders to her collarbones. He traced the high edges, dipped into the hollows and finally started down her chest. When he reached the front clasp of her bra, he raised his gaze to hers and arched an eyebrow in silent question.

Lilli nodded and, as he flicked the clip open, she arched her back, making the sheer-lace cups spring apart and fall to the bed next to her. Her generous mounds were on full display. He'd seen them before. Obscured slightly in photos for a modelling campaign and those horribly blurred shots of her sunbaking topless, but he'd never been privy to firsthand sight. Never within touching distance. She was lush and full, the dark tips puckered tight, whether from her nakedness or his attention he didn't care. All he knew was he had to taste them, feel them pressed against his tongue.

Bending down, he cupped her breast in his hand as he lowered his mouth to the peak. Mac sucked the nipple to the roof of his mouth, held it there with his tongue and increased his suction. Lilli arched into him, thrusting her flesh against his face and he sucked harder. She writhed beneath him and he had to place his hand on her shoulder to keep her on the bed.

"Please," she gasped.

Not letting go of his prize, he glanced up to see her head thrown back, her sleek neck extended. Distracted by the enticing curve, he let her nipple slip free with a wet pop. He stretched out beside her and went to work on sampling her throat. With nips and licks, Mac tormented them both for long minutes before the need to be inside her took over. Pulling back, he used his fingers on her chin to turn her face towards his.

"Lilli. Open your eyes." He waited until she complied. "I need you. I need more."

Fear sliced into his gut and he held his breath while he waited for her answer and thought of the possibility she'd say no. He wanted so much more from her. Far more than he was asking for right now. Far more than either of them was ready to deal with. But for now, he'd take her body—if she let him—and he'd cherish every part of her until she came undone in his arms, and when she lay sated, he'd ask for it all.

LIL'S SENSES WHIRLED. Whether from Mac's touch or the fact he was *finally* touching her she couldn't say and didn't get a chance. The second she nodded Mac groaned and went back to tormenting her with mind-numbing caresses. He nibbled on her neck, sucked and licked her skin as his lips and tongue blazed a trail along her throat to the hollow at the base. All the while, he brushed his hands and fingers across her arms and torso in the most sensual touches she'd ever experienced.

Mac dipped his head lower and pressed his lips to the upper curve of her breast. He followed the rise until his mouth found her nipple. The puckered flesh drew tighter, pulsed with an ache that sent bursts of throbbing demand between her legs. With one pull, Mac sucked the hard bud between his teeth and clamped the tip in place while lashing the inflamed nub with his tongue. Lil's breath hitched, her thighs clenched and she squirmed beneath his devouring mouth as he drove her to the edge of release in seconds.

Her back arched, her breasts thrusting higher as she sought more of his tantalising touch. He groaned against her skin. The sound rumbled over her nerve endings and sent sharp arrows of need into her core. A moan slipped from her throat, raw and needy, the cry one of surrender and want. Lil's fingers curled into the bedding in a desperate effort to hold on, the speed at which her orgasm hurtled towards her unexpected and frightening. It was too much. A cry tore from her throat and she pressed her spine into the mattress, hunched her shoulders in a bid to pull away from the intense sensations Mac's suckling mouth delivered to her over-stimulated nipple.

Lil whimpered and Mac pulled back, letting her flesh slip from his lips with a soft slurp. His gaze met hers and he cupped her jaw in his palm, his fingertips stroking her cheek in gentle sweeps. Rising, he brought his head up until his forehead rested on hers. She squeezed her eyes shut, her chest heaving as she fought to rein in her raging lust. She'd never felt such profound pleasure. Never experienced the savage need thrumming through her veins, clawing at her insides. With every laboured breath, she gained a little sanity, a little control. Their noses bumped and he pressed his mouth to hers in a light kiss.

"Easy, Lilli." He spoke against her lips. "Just breathe, baby."

He caressed her face with one hand while rubbing the back of her neck with the other. As the tension eased, Lil's anxiety was quickly replaced by embarrassment. She was behaving like some teenage virgin, and while technically she *was* a virgin this wasn't the first time she'd made out with a guy. But this was Mackenzie, and nothing about him had ever been simple. Her feelings for Mac had been in a jumbled knot of confusion long before they tangled with his or either of them got naked.

Lil opened her eyes to find Mac watching her. She could see the struggle for control in his gaze, feel it in the tremble of his body against hers, and just like that, her own fight for sanity became easier. Knowing she wasn't the only one caught up in the maelstrom of emotions made her minor freak-out that much more bearable.

Mac rolled them to the side but kept her body flush with his. "I'm sorry."

"Sorry?" Lillian couldn't imagine what he'd have to apologise for. She was the one who'd panicked.

"I'm rushing." He took a deep breath, his shirt rubbing over her sensitive nipples and Lil sucked in a harsh breath of her own. "It's just...I've wanted you for so long. Too long."

Sheer pleasure raced through her at Mac's words. To hear him finally admit that he wanted her was better than the thrill she'd gotten the day she opened Lilli Pond. Lil stiffened. Did he truly hold that much power over her happiness? Before these last few minutes she would have said no, but now... Now she wondered if she'd be able to walk away from Mac after making love with him. And there was no doubt in her mind they would take that last step. Neither of them could walk away from what they'd started all those months ago with one kiss.

"Give me a minute." Mac tightened his hold, tucked her

into his chest as he drew in another deep breath and shuddered. "I want this to last."

Last? Was he talking about sex or them? Lil's mind swirled with doubt. Could this be just sex? She knew it was far more than that for her, but what about Mac? Did he see this as the start or the finish line? What if this was all he offered? Would it be enough?

Mac placed two fingers under her chin and tipped her head back until their gazes locked. He brushed strands of hair from her face, tucking it behind her ear. "I seem to remember offering to kiss you better."

He leaned forward and pressed his mouth to hers. The caress was light, just a quick peck before he pulled away. "Don't move. Stay exactly as you are."

Unsure of his intentions, Lillian remain in place. Rising up on his elbow, he gently stroked his fingers across the bruising dotted down her side. From hip to shoulder, each mark received equal care. When he reached the top, he started back down, but this time he followed his fingertips with his lips, skimming them softly on the sections of discoloured skin. The red mark that spanned the back of her arm and shoulder was barely visible, but Mac treated the spot to his own brand of doctoring. Curling his fingers through hers, he lifted her arm so he could give his attention to the patches running the length from elbow to her wrist.

A shiver stole through her and goose bumps sprang up in its wake as Mac placed a kiss on the inside of her elbow before moving to the final blemish on the edge of her wrist. He shifted lower on the bed and lowered her arm to the mattress in front of her. The position allowed him to reach her ribs. Lost in his ministrations, Lil forgot she lay naked except for her underwear, not that they concealed much. Sheer to the point of being see-through, the silk and lace hid nothing from Mac's gaze.

Slowly, he made his way down her side until he reached the worst of her bruises.

Her hip throbbed to the beat of her heart, but the pain wasn't enough to detract from Mac's obvious concern. Lil had never been on the receiving end of his softer side. She'd seen glimpses when he dealt with his mother, but other than those rare occasions he kept himself in check around her. Always at arm's length. Until seven months ago. Until now. The gentle touch of his lips against her pounding hipbone drew her gaze. He started at the outer edge and worked his way around and to the middle with every circuit his lips took.

Mac gripped her thigh and eased her to her back. He ran his fingers along the edge of her undies while he continued to nuzzle the curve of her hip. Warm air flowed over her lower belly as his mouth followed the path of his hand. His tongue snaked out and dipped beneath her waistband. A trail of fire streaked down, heating her folds and slicking them with moisture. Lil's stomach muscles quivered as he continued to her other hip, and she couldn't stop the moan that gurgled in her throat as he explored every inch of skin between her hipbones.

His lips travelled over the smooth expanse of her stomach as he made his way up her body. He licked and nibbled, sucked and lapped at every dip, every curve. By the time he'd made his way to her breasts, Lillian was breathless. Mac slid his leg between hers as he leaned into her and brought her naked flesh in touch with the clothed length of his. A frustrated cry spilled from her parted lips. She wanted his skin on hers. Wanted to feel his hardness pressed against her from head to toe.

"Clothes off." Her hands pulled at his shirt. "I want to feel you."

He stilled her hands. "No."

Lil froze, her gaze darting to meet his. "No?"

"If I get naked, Lilli, the game is over. I won't be able to resist sinking my cock inside you."

"But I want that," she breathed.

Mac's mouth brushed hers. "Me too, but I want to make it good for you first."

"It is good. Better than anything I ever imagined."

"I want to touch and taste every millimetre of you before I lose myself in you."

"Please, Mac." Lil scrambled for words to convince him. "We'll leave our underwear on but I want to feel you against me. Want to touch you with my hands."

He groaned and dropped his head to her shoulder. Lil took the opportunity to run her hands under his shirt, pushing the fabric up his back and digging her fingers into the hard muscles along his spine.

"Please, Mackenzie." She slid her hands lower, dipped them into the waistband of his jeans. "Get naked with me."

His hips rocked and his erection pressed into her sex, making her gasp as pleasure ricocheted around her lower belly. Arching up, Lil dug her fingers deeper into the steely muscles of his arse. With a growl, Mac straightened his arms and lifted away, forcing her to let go. Frightened he was going to leave, she reached for him, her hand brushing over the bulge beneath his zipper. Moaning, she palmed the hard length, her fingers curling around his girth. Mac shuddered and thrust his cock into her hand. She stroked him through his pants, mapped the head before sliding down to cup his balls.

"Enough," he growled.

She stilled her fingers and raised her gaze to his. "Why—"

Mac rolled away and pushed to his feet. He stood beside the bed, fists clenched, knuckles white, and stared down at her. Nostrils flaring wide, he sucked in a deep breath, and she could see the internal war he waged flare in his eyes. For a moment, Lil felt uneasy. Lying before him with only her see-through underwear covering her she felt exposed—naked in a way even the thickest layer of clothing wouldn't change. But then he moved.

He whipped his shirt over his head and tossed it to the floor. Lil barely had time to admire his sculpted chest and abs before her gaze was drawn to the action below his belt. In seconds, his fingers had the button popped and zipper down. Bending, Mac yanked off his shoes and tossed them aside before standing and shoving his jeans down. She sucked in a breath. The boxer briefs he wore moulded his flesh like a second skin, and the damp patch surrounding the tip of his cock showed her how aroused he was. Add the obvious—and impressive erection—and Lil had no doubt Mac wanted her as much as she wanted him.

Lil got to her knees and crawled towards him. Her nerves were on edge. Anxiety raced under her skin with longing close behind. It was the wanting that gave her the courage to move. To go after the only man who'd ever made her yearn with such desperation. She laid her hand on his chest, splayed her fingers wide and soaked up his warmth. The golden hair dusting his pecs tickled her palm and she savoured the jolt of lust that surged to all her pleasure points. Each breath she took pulled Mac's scent inside her, branding her soul with ease. She'd give him anything he asked, but she knew he wouldn't ask. If she was going to get what she wanted, she'd have to push him until he couldn't say no.

With startling clarity, Lil realised that's exactly what she'd been doing. She'd poked and prodded the sleeping bear until he'd come after her. He'd chased her for months. She knew that. Knew that even with all she'd done to taunt him he still had a grip on his control. It was time to break that last hold. Sliding her hand down Mac's stomach, Lil pushed beneath his briefs and wrapped her fingers around his cock.

6

"LILLI." Her name exploded from his mouth on a rush of air. Blood surged into his groin, filling his cock with urgent need. Another breath hissed through his teeth as Lilli stroked her hand down to his balls and back to the tip. She swept her thumb over the crown and spread the bead of precome oozing from the slit in a slick slide across his straining flesh. *Fuck.* Every muscle quivered with unleashed desire. Years of pent-up emotions bashed against the walls he'd erected, threatening to break free. Mac clenched his jaw, his back teeth grinding together with brutal force. He couldn't afford to lose control. Couldn't allow his desperate need free reign.

She stroked him with her delicate hand and he couldn't resist the urge to glance down—to see her skin moving against his. His sac drew tighter with each slide of her fingers, each squeeze, and he knew no matter how much he wanted to watch her touching him, he was too close to the edge to continue to do so. Mac closed his eyes and let his head fall back to make sure he wouldn't catch sight of her carnal caress even if the temptation to raise his eyelids proved too great. He sucked a breath in through his nose and was slammed with the scent of her. Not the delicate perfume she always wore but the unmistakable aroma of arousal.

He knew the smell. It had coated his fingers twice before. Breathing deeply, Mac pulled in another dose of Lilli. She surrounded him. Inside. Outside. She touched him everywhere, and he was struck by the undeniable urge to touch her in return. All of her. But most of all, he wanted to touch and taste the heart of her where her heat and flavour and scent were strongest. Opening his eyes, he raised his head and looked at her once more. Reaching down, he grabbed her wrist and held her still.

"Enough." He pulled her hand from his cock and nudged her backwards. "My turn."

"But I hardly got—"

"Later." Mac wrapped his hands around her waist, lifted her off her knees and laid her on her back. "Scoot your arse to the edge of the bed."

Mac helped her move to where he wanted and, slipping his fingers into the elastic sides, tugged her underwear down her thighs. Saliva pooled on his tongue as the neatly trimmed dark hair covering her mound was revealed. He had to swallow before he embarrassed himself by drooling. The sight and smell of her caused his heart to pound, his blood to rush. His cock jerked with the added surge of lust and he sank to his knees next to the bed. Her undies tangled on her stilettos, but he quickly untwisted them and tossed them aside. Gripping her ankles, he spread her legs and, placing her feet on his shoulders, moved between her parted thighs.

"My shoes." She tried to tug her legs free.

"Leave them on." He wanted to take her in her fuck-me heels.

Mac ran his fingers over the top of her feet. Traced the tiny bones of her ankles and slid his hands around to smooth his palms up her calves. He thrilled at the shiver that raced over her.

"You look so fucking hot with them and nothing else on." He turned his head, brushed his lips across her silky skin. "I want to taste every inch of you, but I can't wait to eat the best part."

He gave her no more warning before he zeroed in on the lush folds cradled between her legs. Flavour exploded on his tongue. Wet and hot, her musky taste flowed over his tongue and entered his bloodstream like the finest scotch—a smooth burn, it hit his gut in a burst of heat that expanded until it covered him from top to bottom. Mac licked up one side and down the other, curled his tongue around her clit then flicked at the hard knot of nerves. She squirmed beneath him and he wrapped his arms around her thighs to hold her still. Her cream filled his mouth and coated his chin and he greedily lapped up every drop.

"Mac. God. Please."

Lilli thrashed against the bed, but he didn't let up. Instead, he dove deeper. Plunged his tongue into her pulsing pussy and fucked her with it. Her hips bucked, her heels digging into his shoulders as she tried to pull him closer. Mac shrugged and her feet slipped behind him, but that allowed her to cross her ankles and squeeze his head like a vice. Letting go of her thighs, he gripped her knees and tugged them apart. When she eased her hold, he let her legs drop to his sides. The position freed his arms and enabled him to use his hands along with his mouth to drive her over the edge.

Mac pressed his tongue to her clit and slid a finger into her pussy. Lilli jerked at the contact, her walls clamping around his invasion with crushing intensity. He lapped at her and drove his finger in and out with ever-increasing speed. Her channel rippled against him, her tightness sucking at him as he searched for that magic spot. Carefully, he probed with a second finger, but he didn't get more than the tip inside when her climax ripped loose. Hips surging off the bed, she impaled her clasping body on his fingers.

He shuddered as the heat and force of her orgasm washed through her and over him. Impossibly tight, the slick walls of her pussy were snug around his fingers. One finger remained buried to the hilt while the other penetrated with barely the tip. The knuckles of his second finger ached where the digit was bent at an awkward angle. As the last of her convulsions ebbed away, Mac dropped a kiss to the top of her mound and withdrew his hand. Her pussy clutched at his retreating flesh, clinging as though attempting to keep him buried in her depths. Urgency lashed at him. He needed to be inside her.

Shoving his hands into his pants, he pushed them to his thighs and moved into position when the air was stripped from his lungs. *Condom.* Jesus fucking Christ, he didn't have a condom.

"Fuck!" He shot to his feet.

"What?" Lilli's hands reached for his. "What's wrong?"

"I don't have anything. Do you?"

"What?"

Her confusion only escalated his frustration. "Condoms! Do you have some?"

"No." Lilli shook her head and Mac groaned.

"In my room. There's a box in my room." He took a step away but she lunged forward and stopped him.

"I'm on the pill."

Stopped in his tracks, Mac stared at her. He was tempted. *So* tempted. "I never have sex without a condom." Mac didn't add he'd never trusted a woman enough to allow her to take care of protection.

"I haven't had sex without protection either, Mac. I promise you, I'd never lie about this."

Gut deep, he knew he could trust Lilli—wanted to trust her—but his brain had kicked into gear and couldn't quite let go of the rule he'd lived by since he'd lost his virginity in the backseat of his car at seventeen.

Lilli pointed to her beside drawers. "The packet is in there. You can see I've taken all the days. I know that doesn't prove I've taken them correctly but I swear to you, Mackenzie, I would *never* trick you like that."

Mac stepped towards the drawers, his gaze never breaking contact with Lilli's. He was on the verge of a second step when mind and instinct converged. Of course she wouldn't lie to him. She had no reason to trick him, to attempt to trap him. Hell, if either of them were trying to set themselves up for life, it would more likely be him. Lilli had far more at stake than he did.

"Are you sure?" He had to ask. Had to give her every opportunity to back out before he couldn't. Right now he still had enough brain power to go to his room and get the necessary protection, but once he touched her again he'd be lost to everything except her and his need to be buried deep in her hot body.

"I'm sure." Her hand slid against his, her fingers weaving their way through his. "I've never been more certain of anything in my life."

She tugged on his hand, pulled him a step closer to the bed and used her other hand to push his underwear the rest of the way down his legs. Mac cupped her jaw and leaned forward to brush his mouth over hers. It was meant to be a sweet kiss. A soft caress of gratitude, but it rapidly turned urgent. Frantic with need and want, their tongues collided as each of them sought to quench the desire erupting between them.

Mac moved closer and pressed Lilli back against the

mattress as he settled his body over hers. She yielded beneath him. Her softness cradling him in a warm embrace he was helpless to resist. His cock nestled in the slick folds of her pussy and he rocked into her, dragging a moan from both of them. Moisture coated his shaft and he continued to glide along her slit until he risked coming apart before he ever got inside her. But he wanted to be sure she came again, needed her near the edge when he entered her. He desperately wanted to feel her walls contracting around his length as he pounded into her.

"Now, Mac," she panted. "I need."

He tilted his hips and brought his cock to her opening. Wetness coated both of them and his crown pressed inside.

"More." Lilli's heels dug into his arse and he jerk in pain.

She still wore her fuck-me shoes. Mac smiled as he hooked his arms behind her knees and bent her legs against her body. His cock slipped a little deeper, and he sucked in a breath as Lilli moaned, her entrance squeezing him. Bracing his hands on the back of her thighs, Mac leaned back and watched as he withdrew and pushed back in. She hadn't yet taken the tip and her pussy fought him every millimetre of the way. Damn, she was tight.

"Mac. Please."

Dropping her legs, he leaned forward, his chest pressing to hers as he braced his elbows beside her head. He twisted his fingers in her hair and brought his mouth to hers. Rocking his hips, Mac edged in and out of her tightness. With each pass, he slipped a little deeper, and his need to sink to the hilt grew stronger. But the pressure on his cock held him in check. Her body wouldn't give, and for a moment he wondered if this was what she really wanted. But she clawed at his back, her nails scoring his skin, and her need was obvious.

Breaking their kiss, he clenched his jaw and tried to ignore the desperate urge to slam home. Mac flexed his hips and pushed a little farther. The pressure on his cock was mind-blowing, and he was barely inside her. While the wet heat invited him in, her pussy's unyielding walls held him out, and it took every ounce of control he had to ignore the call of his body's desperate desire and respect the struggle of hers.

He eased back again, returned his mouth to hers and licked his way from one side to the other as he flexed his hips and worked his cock in. Unsure if the exhilarating sensations bombarding his groin were due to the lack of condom or her unbelievable tightness, Mac concentrated on teasing her with his tongue while pushing deeper. She wrapped her legs around his thighs, her spiked heels digging in and tugging him closer. Lilli's hands slid down his back to cup his arse and her fingers pressed into the taut muscles, urging him closer still.

She tore her mouth from his, her breath rasping through her teeth as she demanded more. "Deeper. I need." Her fingers and shoes dug into his flank a second before she launched her hips from the mattress and impaled herself on his cock.

The sharp cry of pain, along with the clamping grip of her pussy and rigid body speared Mac's brain with a knowledge he'd failed to comprehend. "Fuck! Shit!" The words ground out through clenched teeth as he tried to pull out.

"No!" Lilli's arms and legs encircled him like bands of steel. "It's okay. I'm okay."

Her body relaxed against him and her breath eased through her nose at a steadier pace. None of it changed the fact that Mac was one hundred percent positive he'd just taken Lilli's virginity. "Why—" His train of thought was derailed. Lilli's pussy rippled along his length and her hips rocked, sliding his cock through her hot wet flesh.

"Oh," Lilli sighed. "Don't stop."

She undulated beneath him, her pelvis driving his cock in and out of her pussy in shallow increments. Sensation swelled.

His balls tucked tight to his groin as his mind was finally drowned out by the lust surging in his veins. He eased out, withdrew until only his tip remained enclosed in heat. Mac fought the need to slam forward. Slowly, he pushed back in, and the razor-sharp edge of need sliced along his nerves while the hot kiss of Lilli's walls glided over his shaft. Her hips bucked against him, her flesh convulsing around him as her body demanded more.

Mac was lost. The scorching touch of her deepest parts sent a lightning bolt of liquid fire up his spine. Jolted by the electrifying throb of hunger that streaked through him, he pistoned his hips, ramming his cock into the channel that finally yielded for him. She moved with him, her body finding the rhythm of his, as he increased the length and speed of his thrusts. He drove deeper with each pass. Faster. Harder. His orgasm roared closer and he slipped his hand between them to search for her clit. Clenching his jaw, he struggled to hold on until she joined him. Determined they'd reach the top together, Mac manipulated the hard bud at the apex of her sex.

Lilli cried out. Her body bucked under his, her nails and heels digging into him with punishing force. Mac circled her clit, rotated his hips as he pulled out, pushed in. She writhed beneath him, her breath hot on his neck where she buried her face against him. The first spasm rippled through her into him and he picked up the pace of his cock and fingers. Lilli's back bowed and her breath stalled on a strangled gasp she held for one heartbeat, two. Then she snapped. A whiplash-quick strike that broke the wave of her release over both of them.

He didn't have time to absorb her body's pleasure before he was swamped by his own. Fire exploded in a shower of sparks. His hips thrashed, his cock pounding in and out as hot pulses of come surged through his shaft and spilled into Lilli's core. Each spurt squeezed his balls and zapped the breath from his lungs.

Mac's muscles trembled, exhausted. Slumping forward, he twisted to the side and took her with him. Holding her tight, he kept their bodies joined as he fought to catch his breath and find his sanity.

~

EVERY BREATH LILLIAN took saturated her senses with Mac. Mac and sex. Hot, wet, mind-blowing sex. She drew in another draft of air and savoured the scent. Her chest no longer heaved, but her heart continued to pound in a fast beat that pumped the lingering throb of her orgasm to all corners of her body. As the pleasure ebbed the dull ache between her legs intensified. The unmistakable pang of tissues stretched farther than ever before served as a reminder of what she hadn't revealed. She'd hoped he wouldn't be able to tell but feared the small cry that had slipped free when she'd experienced the sharp stab of pain as he'd finally entered her had been a dead giveaway.

Lil opened eyelids heavy with exhaustion. She wanted visual memories to go along with the emotional and physical ones. It was worth the effort. His skin glistened with sweat and she breathed deep again. The urge to taste him stole through her and she stuck out her tongue to indulge the desire. She licked the hollow in the base of Mac's throat and the small indent fluttered beneath her tongue. The rhythm matched the thump of his heart that echoed through her breasts where they pressed against his chest. Her blood hummed with the satisfaction of release, but she felt desire rise once more.

Mac stirred, briefly tightening his arms around her before he leaned back and used two fingers to tip her chin up until their gazes met. His eyes swirled with sated arousal and other emotions she didn't want to examine, but the longer he stared at her the more one emotion showed. She watched as satisfaction, desire, happiness, confusion, and finally anger moved through his blue eyes. Lil knew what was coming. Knew he wouldn't be happy he'd taken her virginity—or that she'd neglected to mention it. If only she could find the right words, she might be able to convince him he hadn't taken anything she wasn't willing to give.

She'd been more than willing. Truth was she'd wanted him to be her first, although she doubted he'd be happy to hear that either. And sure, it hadn't been all hearts and flowers with a declaration of love as she'd imagined a million times, but that was because it surpassed any naive fantasy she could conjure up. There had been no shortage of boys, and later men in her life, except none of them had convinced her to make that final step. From the moment her fifteen-year-old heart and body had looked at Mackenzie Harris as something other than her big brother's best friend, Lil's fate had been sealed. All boys and men from then on were held up to that one unattainable measure of a young girl's imagined perfection.

Lil wasn't sure if she'd placed him on a pedestal or if Mac had climbed up onto such a high platform on his own. Or if what she felt was the residual hero worship of a teenager or the love of a woman grown. It had been hard to tell because until she'd moved into this house with him and Lachlan they'd seen very little of each other. Even now, they barely managed a few words a week on average. And yet the bone-deep yearning she felt for him had never diminished. It had only grown stronger. One thing was certain, the emotions Mac stirred couldn't be ignored and far outweighed anything any other man inspired.

He sighed and ran a fingertip along her jaw, up to her temple and back again. "Why didn't you tell me?" The harsh tone of his voice made a lie of his gentle caress.

Lil shrugged. "No point, it wouldn't have changed anything."

Mac jerked back. "What? Of course it would have."

She couldn't think how he might have stopped the small amount of pain she'd suffered, but his next words soon made it clear.

"I never would have touched you if I'd known." He pulled away, rolling to sit on the edge of the bed, his back to her.

A gasp exploded from her lungs as pain lanced her chest. She didn't dare speak, couldn't form words while she tried to catch her breath.

"You should have told me." Mac bent his head and ploughed his fingers through his hair, making it stand on end more than their romp in bed had. "Fuck!"

He shoved to his feet and paced across the room, his fingers curled against his scalp, tugging the matted strands further. "And why the fuck *are* you still a virgin? What's wrong with those men you date? They can't be blind. Hell, the whole world thinks you're fuckable. Are they gay? Stupid? Too in love with themselves to think about loving you?"

Lillian didn't think Mac wanted answers. Not really. His questions were fired at the floor as he marched back and forth. If it wasn't for the angry vibes coming off him, she'd be tempted to enjoy the view. It amazed her that even stark naked he possessed the ability to project menace. Every muscle rippled with strained energy as he stalked the length of her room. She reached for the bedding and tugged it up to cover her nudity. Funny how she felt more exposed now than she had when he'd been face first in her pussy.

A shiver skipped down her spine and goose bumps sprang up on her skin. His anger seemed to accelerate with each step he took, and the euphoria she'd been bathed in since he'd first kissed her slowly leaked away, fear and anger taking its place.

Fear that he wouldn't calm down and anger that he wouldn't have touched her if he'd known about her untouched state. Anger quickly overtook the fear.

"For God's sake, Mac, it's not like you're the only guy I've crawled into bed with." Lil wrapped the sheet around her as she climbed off the bed. She ignored the twinge of sore muscles.

He stopped and pivoted on his heel. His eyes, dark with anger, bore into her. "I think what just happened makes that a lie."

"You don't have to have intercourse to go to bed with someone." She turned her back on him and headed for her bathroom only to be brought up short when he grabbed her makeshift wrap. Glancing over her shoulder, she eyed his hand where it gripped the sheet before bringing her gaze up to meet his. "Let. Go."

"No. Not until you explain," he ground out through clenched teeth.

"I don't have to explain myself, Mackenzie. I don't answer to you." She swung her hips and tried to yank the material from his grasp.

"Are you going to make me show you how wrong you are again?"

Lillian gasped. He wouldn't?

"I see you remember how I proved you wrong last time." Mac smiled as he let her go but neither movement brought her comfort.

"Don't you dare touch me." Lil turned to face him fully.

"Funny, just moments ago you were begging me to touch you." He crossed his arms over his naked chest, one hip cocked to the side. "Among other things."

Her traitorous body buzzed with arousal as the muscles in his biceps flexed. Damn. Did he have to look so gorgeous? Lil couldn't stop her gaze from travelling down his body or lingering on his groin. His cock was no longer at rest and the sight of it lengthening—thickening—had her mouth watering and her pussy clenching.

Mac's smirk turned conceited as he leaned forward. "I could have you begging again in seconds, Lilli."

Her eyes widened and her chest rose as she sucked in a breath. He was right. He could make her beg in seconds. The worst part being her heart and body would welcome his attention. Embrace anything he offered. But her mind knew better. Lil straighten her spine and took a defensive step back. She refused to give in. Not now. Not yet. Anger still rolled off him and she refused to surrender until he saw her virginity as the gift it was. Unfortunately, she had the sinking feeling it would take Mac a long time to come to that conclusion.

"Running again, Lilli?" He matched her step.

She shook her head as she retreated farther.

He arched one brow and followed. "Really?"

Lillian moved before she thought. Spinning around, she dropped the sheet and lunged for the bathroom, slamming the door behind her and throwing the lock before Mac could get his hand on the knob. She leaned back against the timber and closed her eyes. The solid panel vibrated along her spine as Mac bashed on the other side.

"Open the door, Lilli." There was a *bang, bang, bang* on the door. "I'm not going anywhere. I'll be right out here no matter how long you hide out in there."

The pounding stopped and the shuffling of bare feet on carpet grew quieter as Mac moved away. Ear plastered to the door, she tried to work out what he was doing, but no more distinguishable sounds penetrated the thick barrier. He'd gone suspiciously quiet. With a huff, she pushed away and strode across to the clothes basket in the corner. Rummaging through,

Lil found the sweat pants and T-shirt she'd worn yesterday and slipped into them. If he was going to wait her out then she wanted to be fully clothed before she emerged from her hiding spot.

The pants and top offered very little in the way of protection for her heart or peace of mind, but right now she'd take all the help she could get. She could only hope Mac was getting dressed out in her room. If not, Lil would draw on the skills she'd learned over years of modelling, pinpoint a spot behind him and not take her eyes off it. As she slipped the T-shirt over her head, Lil caught a glimpse of herself in the mirror and cringed. Her hair looked like a bird's nest and the little bit of makeup she'd applied earlier was either smudged or gone. Sighing, she reached for a face wipe and cleaned her skin of all cosmetics. Once Mac was dealt with, she'd slip under a quick shower before she rejoined the party.

A twinge of guilt pierced her at the thought of leaving the party for even more time, but she knew Cassie would have everything under control. Still, she felt bad about disappearing for so long already. It had to be at least an hour since she and Mac had come upstairs. Lil really didn't want to deal with Mac now. Not with the house full of people. But there was no getting around it. She'd have to convince him they needed to return to the party. If he wanted an assurance they'd talk tomorrow, then she'd hand him her passport and drivers licence. Hell, she'd hand over her entire handbag and even her house keys if that would help.

Taking a deep breath, she squared her shoulders and opened the door. The sight before her made her pulse race and her palms sweat. He was in the same position as earlier, stretched out on her bed, his back resting on the headboard. Only this time the man didn't have a stitch of clothing on. Lil swallowed over the lump of sand in throat. She licked her lips and focused on the painting above her bed as she moved towards him.

She bent down to pick up Mac's jeans as she made her way across the room and, with a flick of her wrist, she tossed them on the bed. He'd sat forward when she'd walked closer, but now he got to his feet and stepped into his pants. Lillian tried not the think about the fact he was doing so without putting his underwear on first. Her heart kicked it up another notch. Struggling to wet the desert masquerading as her mouth, Lil closed her eyes and took a deep breath. Big mistake. The room smelled of sex. And Mac.

Every nerve ending sparked to life. Blood roared in her ears and heat scorched her skin in a wave of prickly fire. She had to get him out of her room. Had to put space between them. Preferably a few walls, some doors and possibly a flight of stairs. Opening her eyes, Lillian tried to focus on the painting again, but movement drew her gaze. Mac had zipped his pants and just slipped the button through when her feet moved. Charging over, she placed her palm on his chest and pushed.

"Hey!"

"I know we're not done." Lil shoved him again and he stepped back. "But we don't have time to talk it out now." She continued moving towards the bedroom door.

"Lilli, what are you doing?" His fingers wrapped around her wrist and pulled her hand away.

"You need to leave and I need to get back downstairs." Lillian used her free hand to reach around Mac and grab the doorknob. "Please, Mac. I promise we'll deal with us tomorrow."

She had the door open and crowded into him to make him take another couple of steps backwards. His grip on her arm slipped as he stumbled. The staggered steps were enough for his body to clear the doorway and put him in the hall.

"Lilli?"

"Please." She gave him one more shove with the flat of her hand before jumping back and slamming the door shut, flicking the lock as she did.

"Lilli?" Mac called as the door closed.

"Later. I promise." Lil turned and walked towards her bathroom and the shower she needed to take while Mac continued to yell her name and rattle the doorknob.

7

MAC STARED at the closed door as though he could open it by will alone. Lilli hadn't answered him once, and he'd called out at least a dozen times. He clenched his fists. His jaw. What the hell just happened? She'd managed, yet again, to get the better of him. Why was he always finding himself in these situations when it came to Lilli? The woman bamboozled him at every turn. And he didn't want to think about the way she'd sautéed his brain in bed either. Or that she'd been a virgin. He dropped his head, closed his eyes and groaned. How the fuck had that happened?

"Never mind, handsome, I'm sure I can make all your troubles go away."

His eyes snapped open as his head jerked up. Sharp nails raked his back and Mac leaped sideways as a shudder of revulsion tore through him. Swinging around, he came face-to-face with a plastic surgeon's idea of the perfect woman. Of maybe it was her idea, and the money had talked loud enough for the doctor to turn a blind eye to beauty and do what the patient asked. Her lips had that bee-stung look, except they looked more like someone had shoved her whole face in the hive and held it there. He couldn't stop the disgust from showing on his face or in his eyes.

She didn't have the same problem though. Not one flicker of emotion showed on her Botox-filled face, but it was certainly present in her voice. "What? Is *the* Mackenzie Harris too good for me? Too busy getting into Lillian McDermott's pants?"

Before he could form a reply, the woman spun on her skyscraper high heel and charged through the milling partiers crowding the hall. Shit. Lilli was right. They couldn't deal with them until they cleared the house. And that wasn't happening anytime soon. Mac huffed out a breath and turned towards his room. A change of clothes and a few minutes to think were in order, and he wouldn't find either of those out here with the who's who of Australian celebrity-dom.

Heading in the opposite direction to the bottle blonde, Mac strode along the hall. Eyes focused on his door, he ignored the blaring music and those around him and tried to come up with a way to empty the house without setting it on fire. Brushing past a couple pressed against the wall involved in a hot-and-heavy make-out session, he was reminded of Lilli. He'd had her like that more than once tonight and he planned to do it again. Soon. His cock stirred, and he recalled his lack of underwear with a painful jolt. Reaching out, the knob twisted in his hand and he cringed at having left his room unlocked.

A quick glance around showed nothing out of place, but you never could tell so, Mac checked his briefcase. The combination tumblers were still locked tight and his phone was in his... Shit! Patting down each pocket, he confirmed the worst. He'd left the damn thing in Lilli's room. It was probably on the floor where he'd tossed his jeans after stripping out of them. The thought brought back vivid images of Lilli. Naked. Against him. Under him. His cock filled and pressed against the cool metal teeth of his zipper, causing pleasure and pain to meld.

Grinding his teeth and clenching his fists, Mac reined in his wayward hormones and started to formulate a plan. He snatched up the bedside phone and hit speed-dial one. The line rang once before connecting.

"Mr. Harris."

"Put a team together."

"Yes, sir."

"Oh, and bring me a car." Mac undid his jeans and pushed them down his hips with one hand. "I'll be taking Lilli off-site so you'll be in charge."

"I'll have it under control within the hour," Lucas said and hung up.

Mac smiled. He wasn't sure how Cassandra Moreland and her team would take McDermott Security taking over, but it was the least of his worries. The big problem was convincing Lilli to leave. Dropping the phone in its cradle, he stepped out of his jeans and headed for the shower for the second time tonight. Determined to get back downstairs before Lilli, Mac was in and out in less than two minutes. He pulled a clean pair of jeans from a drawer, tossed them towards the bed and quickly searched out a shirt and underwear, which reminded him that his phone wasn't the only thing he'd left in Lilli's room.

Grabbing a backpack from his cupboard, Mac tossed in a couple of sweat pants and shirts before getting dressed. He popped the locks on his briefcase, retrieved his wallet and tucked it in his back pocket. He relocked and stowed his bag, then, shouldering the backpack, he strode from the room and made sure the lock engaged as he left. When he reached Lilli's room, he tried the door but found it locked so he continued on downstairs. The place appeared more crowded, if that was possible, and the noise was still at a dull roar. But he could bear it now knowing he'd be out of here before the hour was up.

After stashing his backpack in the closet under the stairs, ready for a fast getaway, Mac surveyed the mass of gyrating bodies and found the man he was looking for. Head and shoulders above everyone else, Lucas Wilhelm sent out obvious keep-clear vibes without lifting a finger, fluttering an eyelid or uttering a word. Mac pushed through the crowd until he arrived at Lucas's side.

"That was quick," Mac said.

Lucas smiled. "I was down the road. My men are on their way." He raised his hand, a set of keys dangling from his fingers. "It's the Explorer double parked out front."

"Have you seen Lilli?"

"No, I was here two minutes after you called and she hasn't come downstairs yet."

"How do you know...never mind. Just tell me there aren't cameras in the bedrooms."

Lucas arched one eyebrow. "Am I going to need to assign a bodyguard to protect you from Mr. McDermott?"

Mac laughed. "No. Lachlan might not like it, but he'll have to learn to accept it."

Hands rising in the universal stop signal, Lucas said, "I don't want to know."

"Good. I wasn't planning to tell you." Mac saw three men in McDermott security shirts walk through the front door. "The troops have arrived."

Lucas chucked. "That's just the scouts. I've got ten coming in." He glanced at Mac. "Plus the others."

"Have you seen Lachlan? Last time I saw him was a few hours ago." Not that Mac had been looking for his friend.

"Mr. McDermott left the premises with a woman earlier in the evening."

Mac turned to look at Lucas. "He left with Kole?"

"He left with Ms. Winters, yes." Lucas nodded. "I do believe she was known by the name Kole several years ago."

"Wow. He actually left with her?"

"Yes. She even let him drive her car." A smile curled Lucas's lips. "It was interesting watching Mr. McDermott squeeze himself into that Mini."

"I'd love to have seen that." Mac clapped Lucas on the back. "I'm going to throw my bag in the car. If you see Lilli, keep her in sight for me."

"No problem."

As Mac headed out the front door, four more of Lucas's men came across the yard. He recognised all except one, but the familiar insignia of *McDermott Media Corp* blazed brightly over each man's left breast pocket. Nodding at them en masse, he continued to the black Explorer that all but blocked the street. He clicking the fob, opened the rear door and dropped the backpack inside. With the door closed and the locks engaged, he made his way back to the house and the coming argument with Lilli. Mac wasn't fool enough to believe getting her to leave her party would be easy, but he did hope for less of a runaround than she'd already given him tonight.

LILLIAN CHECKED one more time in the mirror. She'd forgone the idea of another dress in favour of calf-length Capri pants in black, a cropped T-shirt in a blue that matched her eyes and a paler blue lace overshirt that tied at the waist. Pleased with the look, Lil scooped Mac's phone up off the floor and headed back to the party. She hadn't been missed. Everything remained in full swing. The games in each room had as many spectators as players. Taking a complete lap of the downstairs, she was rounding the corner of the living room into the hall when she spotted Cassie tearing into a large man Lil had never seen before. Her pint-sized friend didn't seem to be worried about their size difference. She was poking him in the chest to emphasise every word she spoke.

Quickening her pace, Lillian stepped up next them. "Is there a problem?"

The air whooshed from her lungs when the man turned towards her. There, as plain as day on his breast pocket, was the logo for McDermott Security.

"No problem. I was just trying to explain to Ms. Moreland that I'm only doing what I was ordered to do."

"Where's Lucas?" Lil demanded.

"Right here," a familiar voice rumbled behind her.

Lil spun around and came face to chest with Lucas Wilhelm, head of McDermott Security. She always forgot just how tall the man was. Tilting her head back, she met his stony gaze with an icy one of her own. "What are you doing here? And what's with the men?" She gazed around, noticing even more of his men scattered throughout the house.

"Mr. Harris asked—"

"What?" Her gaze snapped back to Lucas's, her eyes narrowing. "Mac had no right to call you, Lucas."

"It is also his house, Ms. McDermott," Lucas tried to argue.

"And that means he gets to call all the shots?" She crossed her arms and glared at him. "Where is he?"

Lillian thought she saw a smile play over Lucas's mouth as he glanced down at her tapping foot. He returned his gaze to hers. "Last time I saw him, he was in the kitchen filling a thermos with coffee."

She didn't have time to think about the absurdity of what Mac had been doing, she was too busy thinking up many varied and painful ways to kill him as she stormed through the house in search of her quarry. Lillian wasn't surprised to find him in the kitchen leaning against the counter like he didn't have a care in the world. She'd seen the pose before. It was his lawyer-shark façade. Good thing she wasn't scared of sharks. Or lawyers.

"How dare you. You had no right. No right at all, Mackenzie Harris." Heat scorched her cheeks and Lil didn't want to think about how red they must be. "This is my party and I say who's invited."

"This is my house as much as yours, Lilli, and I'm not leaving it unsupervised when we go."

"Go?" *What the hell?* "I'm not going anywhere."

"Yes, you are." Mac turned to the counter behind him and picked up the thermos Lucas must have been referring to. "We're getting out of here. We need to talk and that requires just you and me, not five hundred people and the latest dance tracks blasting out at sonic boom levels."

"I told you we'd talk tomorrow and I meant it."

"No. We're talking now. It's well after midnight and the party should be winding down now anyway, so we'll leave Cassie and her team to finish out the evening with Lucas and his men standing guard."

Of all the conceited, controlling, arrogant, manipulative... she'd dealt with domineering men in her life, but Mac's actions topped them. Did he think he had the right to make her decisions for her just because she'd had sex with him? He'd been bossy before, but Lil couldn't remember one instance where he'd interfered enough to set her teeth on edge like this. Emotions swamped her. And undermining them all was a need to do as he asked. She *wanted* to please him. And that just pissed her off more. Lillian McDermott was a take-charge, independent woman who didn't answer to anyone, least of all any man sharing her bed.

"I am not leaving this house, and if you think for one second that you can order me around because I let you into my pants, you're mistaken." Lillian's loud outburst ended with tomblike silence. Glancing around, she saw every eye in the room trained on the two of them. Her face flamed hotter, and when she brought her gaze back to Mac's face he was staring at her with anger flashing in his eyes.

"Now that you've broadcast to the world that we've had sex, you might think twice about wanting to get out of here before the media descends, because you can bet that sexy little arse of yours that this is hitting the airways as we speak." He leaned forward, his mouth a whisper from hers. "Personally, I'd rather keep our relationship private, but I guess you always have preferred centre stage."

Mac stalked off, leaving her in the middle of the kitchen with everyone staring at her. Swallowing back the sting of tears, she took a deep breath and went in the opposite direction to Mac. They both needed to cool off. Okay, *she* needed to calm down. She hadn't really meant what she'd said or thought. Had she? The tangle of emotions inside her was tied in knots so tight she could barely breathe. Ducking into one of the downstairs powder rooms, Lil ran cold water over her wrists before sitting on the closed toilet lid and dropping her head between her knees.

She had no idea how long she stayed there going over and over all that had happened between her and Mac, but continuous knocking on the door finally forced her to get up to leave the sanctuary. Mac was right. The noise was giving her a headache. Of course, that could also be the questions, answers and recriminations thundering along her brainwaves. Her face appeared a little blotchy, but the light layer of makeup she'd put on after her shower held, and with the amount of alcohol consumed this evening, she doubted anyone would notice. Flicking the lock on the door, she had to jump back when the door flew open and a woman rushed inside.

"Oh God. Hafta pee. Hafta pee." A pixie-like woman barged all the way in. Unmindful of the person already in the room, the woman raised the toilet lid and her dress at the same time.

Quickly skirting around the door and leaving the busting woman to her business, Lil made her way through the crowd towards the front door. Mac stood with his back to her, Lucas at his side. Her step faltered and she took a moment to catch her breath. Her heart beat double time when he turned in her direction and their gazes connected. Even when she was mad at him, she found him gorgeous. And no matter how he'd gone about it, she did want to go somewhere quiet and be alone with him.

Lil started walking again, her gaze never leaving his. When she reached Mac's side, she placed her hand in his and turned to Lucas. "Let Cassie finish out the night like we'd planned. She's good at her job and doesn't need you or your men interfering, but I'll be grateful if you stay to keep an eye on things regardless."

"Sure thing, Ms. McDermott," Lucas answered. "And Cassie, she's the short brunette, yes? The one with an attitude?"

"I'm not the only one with an attitude, mister." Cassie stepped up beside Lillian. "I take it you're cutting out?"

Lil glanced at Mac. "Yes. I'm done."

"I know. And about damn time too." Cassie wrapped her arms around Lillian and gave her a hug. "Ring me next week and we'll get together for lunch."

"I will. And thanks." Lillian gave Cassie an extra squeeze. "For everything."

"My pleasure. It's been a big learning curve, but I think all the glitches were minor and didn't affect the overall party. I'll email you my staff report on Monday."

"I told you I don't need to see that," Lil said.

"I know, but I'm actually hoping you'll take pity on me again and give your opinion of tonight and what everyone recounts."

"Sure." Lillian offered her friend a smile before turning back to Mac. She really was done with her old life and now she couldn't get away fast enough. "Let's go."

EVERY TIME they made a step towards the door someone snagged Lilli for a chat. While the whole exercise of leaving frustrated the hell out of Mac, it gave him a chance to observe the side of Lilli he admired. She was courteous, giving each person her undivided attention, making it appear as though they were the centre of her world. Not once did she let on that the effort wore on her. But Mac noted the fatigue in her eyes, the slight dip in her shoulders, the slouch in her posture. That's when he stepped in and ushered her from the house, allowing them to make their escape.

He led Lilli across the yard to the black four-wheel drive parked in the street and wondered what had convinced her to leave. The sudden change of mind didn't fit, but then neither did the emotional outbursts they'd both experienced this evening. Lilli slowed, one finely shaped eyebrow arched, but she didn't verbalise the obvious question. Instead, when he opened the door, she climbed up into the passenger seat. Shrouded in silence, Mac navigated the dark streets. Numerous times he thought about breaking the quiet, but each glance in her direction convinced him to give her—and himself—more time before starting the conversation they needed to have.

He couldn't bring himself to initiate the discussion when inch by inch Lilli had shrunk into the passenger seat beside him. Like a helium balloon losing its lift in the days following a party, Lilli deflated by slow degrees. Her enthusiasm, her energy—her happiness—all seemed to seep out of her, leaving her slumped against the soft leather cushion. They were about halfway to their destination and Mac decided to keep quiet until they arrived. The early hours of the morning meant traffic was light and a journey that would normally take an hour took less than forty minutes. Before he knew it, he'd pulled into the driveway of his parents' weekender.

The house was small and old, but it sat perched on a sheltered beach among homes of similar standing. An older neighbourhood not yet bought out and rebuilt by the young and rich, the place offered a sanctuary within spitting distance of the hustle and bustle of busy city life. He'd been more than surprised when his father had showed the house to him and Alec. Mac's parents had spent very little of their lottery winnings over the years, and other than his mother's new car and their sons' education, this property had been their only large purchase. Regardless of their newfound wealth, his parents had continued to live their humble lives in the working-class suburb they'd moved to as newlyweds.

Right now, sitting in the car, staring at the dark, quiet house, Mac thanked his lucky stars they'd seen fit to buy this little getaway. He switched off the engine and turned to face Lilli. Her eyes were closed and her chest rose and fell with even breathes. She'd fallen asleep. Smiling, Mac eased his door open and closed it softly behind him. Skirting the front of the car, he made his way around to Lilli. With care, he popped the door and tried not to startle her. The seat belt clicked free with ease and he slid his arms around her, one behind her back, the other under her knees. He lifted her out of the car and used his hip to bump the door shut before walking down the path to the front door.

As he struggled to get the key from its hiding spot, Lilli stirred. Forced to lean on the wall or fall on his arse, he pressed against the rough timber siding with his shoulder and managed to keep his feet under them, but he lost his grip on her legs and her feet dropped to the floor. Her arms slipped around his neck as she turned in his embrace. Eyes on his, she watched him. The darkness made it difficult to discern her emotions, and for several heartbeats they stood frozen, caught in a silent moment neither appeared willing to break. The kick of a breeze rushing through the trees snapped the spell. Lilli unhooked her arms and, placing her hands on his chest, pushed away.

"You can let go. I can stand on my own." Her voice, husky with sleep, whispered over his skin like a soft caress, and he shivered.

Mac took a step back, retrieved the key without a word and opened the door. Reaching inside, he flicked on the light and gestured for her to precede him. The living room spread out in front of them, the wall of windows directly opposite offering a view of the moonlit bay beyond. In daylight the sun spilled into the room and the waters of North Harbour could be seen rolling in against the shore that butted up to the yard. Night or day, it was a beautiful sight.

"The bedroom is down the hall, the bathroom off it." Mac closed the door behind him. "I'll see what's in the kitchen, but Mum usually has the basics on hand so I can make us something to eat, and there's always the thermos of coffee if you want some."

"No, thanks. I'm exhausted."

Fatigue laced her words. Her eyelids drooped and her movements were slow as she ventured farther into the house. Mac's protective instincts fired to life and, determined to take care of her and give her all she needed, he walked over to the bedroom door and pushed it open.

"Why don't you take a shower and climb into bed. There are spare toiletries and clean towels in the bathroom and the bed is already made up." He stepped back and let her pass. "I'll just duck out to get my bag."

"Bag?"

"I brought a change of clothes. I grabbed sweat pants and a T-shirt for you too."

"Oh, okay." Lilli entered the room only to immediately turn back around. "I almost forgot." She shoved her hand down the front of her top and pulled his phone out of her bra strap. "Here. You left this in my room earlier."

The unintentional reminder of their encounter had colourful images flashing across Mac's mind. Every second of their time together was engraved in his memory banks. The scent and feel of her skin. The flex and give of her body beneath his. Each moan. Every sigh. A shuddered racked him. Warmth surged through his blood, pumping need into his balls, filling his cock and driving his arousal higher. Not wanting her to see his body's reaction, Mac quickly took his phone and turned away.

He went back into the cold morning air and drew in a deep breath. As much as he'd like a repeat tangle with Lilli, they needed to sort things out first. Mac wanted to be sure they were on the same page. This wasn't a casual affair for him. He'd spent years pushing his feelings and desire for Lilli into the dark corners of his mind and heart, but now that he'd let them out there was no hiding from them. Before they left his parents' house she'd be in no doubt that he wanted more than her body.

The problem was he didn't have the first clue where to start in pleading his case. He'd never had to fight for something as important as his relationship with Lilli. Mac brought the phone in his hand up and scrolled through his address book. He couldn't ring Lachlan. There was no way he wanted to discuss the best way to convince Lilli to take a chance on him with her brother. Instead, he pulled up Alec's details and hit call with no regard for the time of day.

LILLIAN WOKE to sunshine and snoring. The sunshine was expected, but the snoring... It took a moment for her sleep-fogged mind to remember where she was, but once the gears engaged there was no stopping the memories of last night taking over. Or the awareness of Mac sleeping beside her. Trying not to disturb him, she turned and took advantage of this rare moment to study him more closely. Asleep, he appeared different. The stress lines around his eyes and mouth were less pronounced, and the worry crinkles he often sported in his forehead were gone too. He looked relaxed—unguarded—in a way she'd never seen him.

The tough, take-no-prisoners lawyer he showed to the world had been put away. Instead, she gazed at an everyday average guy. He could be any man she might have hooked up with over the years. But this was Mackenzie Harris. Her brother's best friend. McDermott Media Corp's top legal eagle. The man she'd spent ten years wanting. And now she had him.

So why didn't she feel like jumping for joy? Why was her heart sitting like an anvil in her chest? Lillian McDermott finally had her heart's desires. A successful business she'd built on her own from the ground up. A modelling career firmly in the past and the only man to stir desire so great it proved hard to think was in her bed.

Or he had been.

Now they were in a strange house—strange bed—and

neither of them were naked. The last thing she remembered was dressing in the sweat pants and shirt Mac had given her and crawling into bed. Alone. At some point he'd joined her, but he hadn't slipped beneath the covers or removed his clothes. He lay on top of the quilt in the jeans and top he'd worn last night. His shoes were off and he'd undone the button and zip on his pants, but that was as far as he'd gone.

His shirt stopped at the edge of his waistband, hiding his midsection from view. A small section of black fabric showed between the gaping sides of his zipper. No glimpse of skin though. Lil wasn't sure if she was pleased or disappointed he'd put on underwear. Or that he'd gotten into bed with her and not taken advantage of the situation. Honesty forced her to admit there would be no advantage taking. She'd give herself willingly and knew it. The question was, did Mac? And if he did, would he want her?

Her gaze moved up his torso, over the lean form hidden beneath the thin layer of cloth, up to the tanned skin of his neck, onto the dark stubble shading his jaw line, and finally to the deep blue eyes watching her. Lil's heart jolted and a lump formed in her throat. Mac's eyes gave no clue as to his mood, but when the corners of his lips curled up in the beginning of a smile, she breathed a sigh of relief.

"Morning." Mac's voice rumbled, his usual deep tones made a little rougher by sleep.

"Morning." Unsure of what else to say, Lil went with the easiest part of the last twenty-four hours. "Where are we?"

"Mum and Dad's weekend place."

Lil turned her head to take a better look at the room.

"I know it's not much, but it's perfect for them and more of an investment really."

His words sounded like an apology, but she hadn't a clue what he should be sorry for. She hadn't managed a good look when they arrived, and now she took the time to examine her surroundings. The furniture was solid pine, the timber blinds the sun streamed through the same golden colour. Cool cotton brushed against her skin as she turned over. The sheets were white, the quilt a marbled pattern of blues, greens and white. Bedside lamps of dark blue powder-coated metal finished off the furnishings. Lil didn't think a designer had ever seen the room but that didn't matter, whoever had decorated this space knew what they were doing.

"It's beautiful." She brought her gaze back to meet Mac's. "Did your mum do this?"

"Yeah." He smiled. "She redid the whole house when they first bought it."

"If this room is anything to go by, the place must be gorgeous. It's...restful." Lillian couldn't think of a better way to describe the ambience of the room. Even with the bright sunshine flooding the space, it felt calm, soothing.

Mac's smiled widened, his straight teeth flashing. "She did a great job. I don't come here often, but I'm always happy to arrive and refreshed when I leave."

He rolled over and pushed off the bed. Unselfconsciously doing up his jeans, he said, "Come on. I'll show you the rest of the house and we'll get something to eat."

As much as Lillian wanted to find out where she stood now that they'd slept together, she was more than happy to ignore the elephant in the corner for a while longer. Her emotions, not to mention her libido, were supercharged. Until she managed to make heads or tails of those, she couldn't deal with Mac's. Not that he appeared ready to offer any of his thoughts. He might look as though he wasn't worried, but Lil knew him well enough to know otherwise. His wooden movements and the small frown marring his kissable mouth were definite giveaways.

For now, she'd take his lead and see what happened. However, there was only so long she'd allow them to pretend nothing was going on. She might not have her bearings yet but she would soon, and once she did she'd face the shift in their relationship head-on. Like every other aspect of her life, this new development would be dealt with in the usual way, with determination and precision. Lillian was single-minded when it came to what she wanted. And she wanted Mackenzie Harris.

8

MAC SLIPPED his phone back into his pocket.

"You're not going to answer that?" Lilli took a sip of her coffee.

"No."

He wasn't about to reveal it was Lachlan. Again. Judging by all the missed calls, the man had been ringing Mac all night. He'd barely turned his phone back on when, along with the manic beeping of voicemail messages, his best friend was once again trying to reach him. One more thing he was reluctant to deal with. Mac had never encountered this side of himself. Putting things off had never been a trait until today. Today he didn't want to deal with anyone or anything. Unfortunately, he didn't have the luxury of putting either his changing relationship with Lilli or his best friend's urgent need to contact him aside.

"If it's work, you should see what they want. Don't put it off because of me."

"It's Lachlan."

"Oh."

"Yeah." Mac grimaced. "My thoughts exactly."

"What does he want?" Lilli placed her mug on the table, the slight trembling of her hand giving away her anxiety as much as the wobble in her voice.

"It doesn't have to be about what you're thinking." He wanted to calm her fears, but if he was honest, and he planned to be truthful with her from now on, he had to tell her how he felt about Lachlan's reaction to them being together. "And even if it is, it's none of his business, and I plan to tell him so. What happens between us stays between us. Your brother can like it or lump it."

"I get the feeling he'll be in the lump it camp."

Mac shrugged. "So be it."

"You should probably see what he wants." She gestured towards his pocket. "If it's about us, hand the phone to me and I'll talk to him."

He smiled. There weren't many people in this world willing to deal with an agitated Lachlan McDermott, but Lilli wouldn't hesitate to take on the big brother she'd spent her life getting around. From the minute he'd met the McDermott siblings, Mac had known Lachlan's one Achilles's heel was his baby sister. His friend wasn't exactly a pushover where she was concerned, but Lilli was more than a match for Lachlan. They both had the mile-wide McDermott stubborn streak.

"Fine." He retrieved his phone. "I'll listen to the ten messages first. But I'm not returning his call unless it's something other than you and me he wants to talk about."

"Okay. Put it on speaker so I can listen."

The first few messages were Lachlan swearing about a photographer and a runaway ex-model. Each message quickly deteriorated into his best friend threatening to do Mac harm if he didn't answer his phone. In the final message Lachlan confessed to using Lillian's phone to find Cameron's address and phone number. Before he could stop her, Lilli snatched the phone from the table and after a few swipes of her finger she brought the device to her ear.

"What the hell is going on, Lachlan? Call me as soon as you get this."

Lilli pulled the phone from her ear and stabbed at the screen with the side of her index finger, her long nail clicking against the glass. Again she put the device to her ear, only this time she didn't leave a message, she simply ended the call and hit redial after a minute. Finally, she gave up and dropped the phone on the table.

"He's not answering? He rang only a minute ago," Mac said.

"Do your parents have a computer here?"

"No, why?"

"Never mind." She pushed back her chair and stood. "I bet I can find what I'm after on the TV. They've got Foxtel, right?"

Mac scrambled to his feet and, grabbing his phone, followed Lilli into the house. She'd already switched on the television and was madly flicking through the channels.

"What are you looking for?"

Lilli gasped and the images on the screen stopped flashing by. Instead, a dark, grainy image of two people making out filled the forty-two-inch plasma panel.

"Holy shit!"

"Holy shit is right." Lilli tossed the remote control on the couch.

"No wonder Lachlan was threatening me with death."

Mac stopped staring at the television to stare at his phone. With practiced ease, he pulled up a search engine and plugged in the necessary terms. What greeted him made his gut churn and bile rise in his throat. There were images of Lachlan and Kole all over the media.

"Fucking hell."

"What? What? Show me." Lilli grabbed his wrist and turned the phone in her direction. "Wow."

"Wow doesn't cover it."

"I have to ring Cam."

Once again, she was too quick for him. Lilli snatched the phone out of his hand and was madly tapping at the screen. She walked away, putting the device to her ear as she went. Disappearing into the bedroom, she closed the door behind her, effectively shutting him out. Mac wasn't sure he liked being excluded, but right now he needed to know if he had to go into damage control, except without his phone or a computer his hands were tied. He used the only resource at his disposal and, picking up the remote, began flicking through the channels until he found a twenty-four-hour news network. It made him sick to think the station flashing up blurred, dark images of his boss and the legendary Kole was owned by McDermott Media Corp.

Mac turned away. He'd seen enough for now. Besides, there was little he could do here without a computer or his phone. He went to tidy up their breakfast dishes while he waited for Lilli to finish her call. It didn't take long to clean up, and he was back in the living room in front of the TV when Lilli came out of the bedroom and handed him the phone. Her gaze glued to the television and one of numerous pictures of Lachlan and Kole being shown.

"I'm not sure what went on last night, but Lachlan is with Cam and I don't think he wants to talk to either of us right now. He hung up on me."

"He did?" For a second, Mac wondered if he should leave it alone, except he couldn't. "What did he say before he hung up?"

"We've both got some explaining to do."

"We have?" Mac laughed and gestured at the television. "Somehow I don't think we're the only ones."

"No. And I got nothing out of Cam before Lachlan grabbed the phone and hung up. Is that Gabriella?" She pointed to the muted TV.

Mac glanced at the screen. Great. They were rerunning the press conference Lilli's mother had given earlier today. "Yeah, she let the world know Lachlan had a thing for Kole when he was a teenager."

"Amazing how when the shit hits the fan Gabriella always manages to float to the top." Lilli's lips pressed together in a tight line of disapproval, the bottom one protruding slightly, and Mac had the urge to lean forward and lick the enticingly plump flesh.

In spite of the chaos unfolding around them, he was instantly thrown back into the desperation of wanting Lilli. The grinding frustration of craving something he shouldn't. Only she wasn't off-limits anymore. They'd already crossed the line and there was no going back. He took a step closer before his brain kicked into gear and reminded him they hadn't talked. Hadn't cleared the air or the way for them to move forward.

"Why do you keep pulling back? What could possibly stop you from doing what you want, Mac? I know it isn't me."

He met her gaze, and for the life of him he couldn't think of a word to say. Him, the man who made a living from knowing the right words for every occasion.

She shook her head. "Is it because you were my first? I never planned it that way. I've been with other guys—"

Mac held up his hand. "Stop right there. I know we need to talk but I'm not interested in talking about that. I don't want to know why none of them hit a home run. I'm still angry you didn't tell me, but I think I understand why you chose not to reveal your virginal state."

"Jesus, Mac. You make it sound like I was the Virgin Mary."

"That's not what I meant." Mac shook his head in frustration. "Dammit, Lilli, I want to talk but not about sex."

"Was it bad?"

Mac's jaw dropped. "Bad?" She couldn't be serious.

"It's not the first time you've given me the impression I'm not up to par on the sexual front."

"What?" He clenched his fists so he wouldn't wrap his hands around her throat and shake her. "Lilli, you're above par on every front, and just because you're somewhat of a novice, don't for one minute think your sexual skills are any different."

"Oh?"

He dragged a hand down his face. "Jesus Christ, woman, you drive me insane."

"That can't be good either. Aren't I supposed to inspire hearts and flowers?" The corner of her mouth twitched.

Mac narrowed his eyes. "Are you laughing at me?"

Her face lost all expression, took on the emotionless mask he'd seen over and over on numerous photographs throughout the years. "No. What do I have to laugh at? First my kiss is bad, but you chose to repeat the action anyway. Then sex with me made you angry and you don't want to talk about it, so I assume that was bad too. And now I drive you crazy. Nope. Nothing to laugh at here."

When she put it that way, he really did sound insane. And maybe he was. Crazy about the woman in front of him. The one he'd kept at arm's length for too many years to count. For reasons he failed to remember now. He knew he loved her, had since he'd met her, but that love had changed—matured—as they'd grown older. Now he wanted to know if what he felt, what she felt—and he was in no doubt she felt something—if what they had could be more. So much more than either of them could imagine.

"I want you." He couldn't hold the words back.

Lilli smiled, her gaze sliding down his body. "Ditto."

"No. Not in bed. Well, yes, in bed, but not yet. I want more." Mac ran his fingers through his hair. "I want it all. With you."

"What exactly are you saying, Mac, because you'll have to spell it out for me here. I've spent too many years getting the brush-off or being ignored or ordered around to leave anything to chance."

He could understand that. Their relationship had been volatile to say the least. The fact that unpredictability had exploded into the best sex of his life had to mean something. Didn't it? Surely she knew that. She had to know he wanted to take their connection deeper on every level. Take it all the way.

"I want to date." The words burst from his mouth before he thought them, but once they had, it all became clear. "I want to take you out to dinner. The movies. Go for walks on the beach, in the park. Take you away for quiet weekends, just the two of us. Sit on the couch and watch the news. Make dinner together. Dance under the stars. I want to go back to the beginning. Do this right."

"That could take awhile."

"I've got the time."

"We might not get it right."

"Sure, we may fuck up along the way. Hell, I'm a man. It's guaranteed I'll fuck something up. Just look at how stupid I've been up until now."

"You haven't been that dumb."

Mac smiled. "I notice you're not completely denying my stupidity."

"I believe in taking responsibility for one's mistakes."

"Speaking of responsibilities, we should head home and clean up before we do anything else."

"We?" Lilli arched an eyebrow. "You're offering to help?"

Grinning, he said, "Sure. I'll tell you want needs to be done."

Laughter spilled from her lips and she slapped him on the arm. "Lucky for you I've got it all under control without the necessity of lifting a finger."

"Oh? How so?"

"Cassie had her crew cleaning up as we went last night and she would have had the house put back to rights before leaving this morning."

"So we'll be going home to a clean, *empty* house?" Mac would have helped, but relief swamped him as he thought of going home and not being faced with utter chaos.

"I'm not as irresponsible as you think."

"I never thought... Okay, fine, I may have entertained the idea that you did some careless things." He shrugged. "It's the image you project, whether you mean to or not."

"Oh, I meant too."

Mac shook his head. "You'll explain that to me one of these days. On one of those long walks we're going to take. But right now, let's go home. There's no point putting off the fallout from your party any longer. Lachlan will have my arse if I don't shut down the media circus currently in full swing."

He held out his hand, and when Lilli slipped her fingers through his he led her to the bedroom to collect their things, his mind already planning their first date, a romantic dinner with a kiss good night at the door. Tonight was the perfect time to start.

~

THE SECOND they entered the house, Mac began mumbling about Lachlan, photographers and damage control. He settled in the kitchen with his phone and laptop and barely made a peep when she offered him a drink. Taking the hint, Lillian went upstairs to shower and change. Refreshed, she tried to reach Cam again, but her friend wasn't answering. Lil wasn't up to a confrontation with her brother just yet so she didn't bother calling him. Lachlan would find her soon enough. With nothing else to do, she set out to take stock of the party's aftermath.

Walking through every room of the house, Lillian checked order had been restored. She didn't find one thing out of place, broken or missing. Cassie and her crew had done an amazing job, and Lil sent her friend a text telling her so. The few valuables she'd locked away yesterday were easily returned to their rightful spots, and if Lil hadn't attended the party herself, she might not believe it had ever happened. In fact, unless they'd witnessed the event themselves, no one would guess the place had held a mass of people only hours ago. Arriving back in the kitchen, she found Mac, head bent to his laptop and phone to his ear. He hadn't moved.

She watched him work. The corporate lawyer was out in full force and she couldn't help the shaft of arousal that shot through her belly and down to her core. He hadn't done more than hold her hand since last night and she was beginning to think he would never touch her again at this rate. It was time to get his attention. Lil kicked off her shoes as she walked towards him. When she reached his side, she unbuttoned her denim skirt and lowered the zipper. Pushing it down, she let it fall to the floor and pool at her feet. The only covering below her waist was a thin scrap of lace that masqueraded as thong panties. Her top came next. The straps slipped from her shoulders to her elbows with a flick of her fingers, revealing her naked breasts.

Mac had stopped talking when her skirt dropped but he found his voice long enough to snap into the phone, "I'll call you back."

He disconnected the call and shut his laptop as he stood. With a roughness that thrilled her, he pulled her against him. Caught by her top and his arms now wrapped around her, Lil leaned into him and rubbed her breasts on his chest, making her nipples tingle and tighten. His mouth crushed hers. Lips parted and tongues stroked in hard lashes that spoke of desperation. She clawed at his back, tugging at the cloth separating his skin from her touch. Scrunching the fabric in her fists, Lil pulled the shirt from his pants, wadded the material into a ball and finally put her fingers on warm flesh.

Lillian tore her mouth from his. "Off. Take it off."

Mac abruptly let her go and stepped back. He crossed his arms over his abdomen and gripped the hem of his shirt. In a flash, he had the top off and tossed aside. He put his hands on her waist and lifted her onto the table. The cold surface against her bare skin stole her breath and sent a shiver up her spine. But she didn't have time to protest before Mac's head descended, his mouth laying claim to hers again. Their kiss was no less frantic than before. Driven by a desire restrained for hours, neither of them could hold back now.

Tongues duelled. Hands and fingers explored. Lil parted her legs and Mac stepped between her spread thighs, bringing the bulge straining for release in his pants in contact with her sex. She ground against him, sought relief from the fire building inside her. He rocked into her, his cock stroking along her slit, pressing on the knot of nerves swollen and pulsing with need. Blood rushed through her veins, bells rang in her ears, and Lil clung to the edge, desperate to let go.

The ringing intensified and Mac jumped back, breaking all contact, leaving her crying out in frustration. His chest heaved as he dragged in air, the harsh rasp of his breath filling the room. Lil's lungs struggled to catch air and goose bumps broke out on her skin in a wave that rolled from head to toe. It took a moment for her to realise the ringing in her ears was the doorbell and Mac's phone buzzing at the same time.

"Shit!" Mac ran the fingers of one hand through his hair while reaching for the phone with the other. "Dammit, I didn't want to do that."

Didn't want to what? Kiss her? Touch her? A chill swept through her and she crossed her arms over her breasts.

He glanced at the screen before dropping the phone back to the table. "We shouldn't have done that. It's not what I want."

Mac didn't want her? "But I thought—"

He glanced her way, confusion and lust swirling in his eyes before they widened in panic.

"Oh, no. That's not what I meant." He stepped forward and slipped his arms around her. "I want you, there's no denying that, but I want to get to know you before we jump back into bed."

"What?" Was the man insane? Did he honestly think they'd be able to stay out of bed now that they'd been there? "You can't be serious?"

"Very. I don't want sex interfering or confusing things."

The doorbell buzzed again and Mac let her go once more. "Let me get that."

Lillian didn't have time to argue and her state of undress meant she couldn't follow either. She hopped off the table and pulled her top back into place. Bending down, she scooped her skirt from the floor and stepped into it. As she fastened the button, Mac returned carrying a box piled high with an assortment of groceries.

"What's all this?" Lil asked as she walked over to the counter where he'd begun unpacking fresh vegetables, a packet of steaks and what looked like chicken breasts, wine.

"Dinner." Mac opened the fridge and started putting away the food. "I was planning to take you out, however, after seeing all the media coverage of the McDermott siblings across all medium of broadcasting, I decided it would prove too difficult to enjoy a quiet get-to-know-you meal. So I decided to bring the fine dining to us."

Lil sighed. "We already know each other, Mac."

He spun around and, using the bunch of asparagus in his hand, he pointed at her. "No, we don't. I don't know your favourite food, what movies you like to watch, what your favourite book or colour is. Do you like summer or winter? Baths or showers? Do you sleep naked or clothed?"

"Strawberries dipped in chocolate, romantic comedies, can't pick one book, but romance is my favourite genre. I'm partial to blue, no particular shade. I love all seasons, the change in colours and clothes as much as lying on the beach or sitting by a roaring fire. I love scented baths but rarely have time to indulge. I sleep naked at home and have a favourite shirt I wear when away."

"Why did you never sleep with any of the men you dated?"

Wow. Where did that come from? "I didn't think you wanted to go there."

"Changed my mind." Mac turned and put the asparagus in the crisper drawer.

Lillian shrugged. "Never wanted to."

"But you've been to bed with some of them?" he asked as he shut the fridge.

"Mac." Why was he pushing this now? He'd already voiced his disinterest in her previous partners.

He crossed his arms and leaned against the counter. "Did you wait for me?"

～

MAC HELD his breath while he waited for Lilli to answer. He didn't know why he'd asked or why he wanted to know so badly. Didn't even know what he wanted her to say.

"No." She shook her head. "Not consciously anyway."

"What do you mean by that?"

"I've had a crush on you for ten years, Mac."

"You never said anything."

"If I had, what would you have done? What would you have said, Mac, to a teenager crushing on her older brother's best friend?"

"I don't know." He couldn't quite get his mind around the fact they'd both wanted and missed out on so much because neither of them could be honest, with themselves or each other. Sure, she'd been a teenager at first, but what about the last five years? Why hadn't she said anything before now? He'd be damned if he'd let anything hold them back from now on. "No more hiding. I don't want to miss out on any more time. And I hate knowing you put your life on hold waiting for me."

Lilli smiled. "Don't flatter yourself, Mac. My feelings obviously affected my choices, but I didn't deliberately set out to save myself for you. No one ever inspired the level of desire you do, and what they did was never enough to take that last step. But don't be fooled into thinking I've gone without. I'm far from sexually deprived."

Mac held up his hands. He didn't want to hear details. "Enough."

Lilli's laughter filled the air. "I wasn't planning to give you a blow-by-blow account, Mac, same as I'll never ask about your previous bedmates."

He didn't have to worry about that. His last girlfriend, if a two-week relationship earned her the title, was long gone. Seven months gone. Come to think of it, the last few years had been barren on the dating front, but then he'd put his life on hold to help Lachlan with the takeover and re-shuffle of McDermott Media Corp when the senior McDermott was removed from power. Mac didn't want to be on pause any longer. Life with Lilli waited, and he planned to enjoy every moment of it.

"There wouldn't be much to tell anyway. Like you, I've spent most of my time on my career. McDermott Media has taken up a lot of time and energy, but then you know that."

"Yes, I do. The question is whether you're able to fit dating me into your busy schedule."

"I'll make time." His phone chose that moment to ring. "Starting with switching off my phone."

He walked over to the table, but before he could stop himself he glanced at the screen and saw Lachlan's smiling face. "Well, shit."

"What?" Lilli came to stand next to him. "I'll answer it."

"No." He was too slow. Again. She had the phone to her ear before he could stop her.

"Hey, big brother, what did you screw up now and where is Cam?"

Mac couldn't make out Lachlan's end of the conversation, but Lilli's gave him a pretty good idea about his best friend's lack of success when it came to Cameron Winters.

"Exactly," Lilli yelled into the phone. "You caused the problem, now you have to fix it!"

Thinking better of hanging over Lilli's shoulder while she

and Lachlan got into it, Mac went back to sorting through the box one of Lucas's men had delivered. He'd given Lucas a list of things he wanted and true to form, the man had come through. Mac put the bottle of white wine in to chill and left the red on the countertop, he'd open that later depending on whether he cooked the chicken or the steak. Lilli's voice had softened and he knew whatever anger she'd had towards her brother had ebbed away. They never stayed mad at each other for long.

After everything was put away, Mac took the empty box to the laundry. He was reminded of Lilli's altercation with the drunken Aaron Watson and made a mental note to send the guy a bill for her damaged dress. The torn dress made him think of her bruises and the fact he hadn't checked to see if they were worse today. She hadn't appeared to be in any pain, so Mac could only assume her injuries were minor, although the one on her hip worried him. A soak in the hot tub might help any lingering aches, and Lilli did say she was partial to scented baths. The tub wasn't quite the same, but maybe he could convince her to relax with a glass of wine before dinner.

When he returned to the kitchen, Lilli was nowhere to be seen. He headed to the back deck with the aim of switching on the tub before going in search of her. Only he didn't have to look far. She sat at the top of the stairs leading off the deck. Her elbows were braced on her knees, her fingers twisted together while she stared off into the distance. The way she'd hunch in on herself had him a little concerned, and he wondered if everything was all right with Lachlan and Cameron.

Mac sat beside her and mimicked her pose. "Everything okay?"

She didn't look at him. "Mother came out of the woodwork."

Ah. He wondered when she'd bring up Gabriella's appearance. "I know."

"Why does she do that? Why does she have to make everything sordid or about her? Can't she just disappear forever?"

"Lilli, she's your mother. You don't really want her to disappear." Mac reached over and placed his hand over hers.

Lilli laughed, but the sound wasn't a happy one. "Yes, I do."

She turned to face him. "She never wanted me, Mac. She got pregnant to trap Dad. Everyone knows that. And he never wanted me either. I was an inconvenience, a situation to be dealt with, and everyone knows how Roland McDermott fixes things. Throw a heap of money on it and if the problem won't go away at least it'll be happy for a while."

"Why the sudden self-pity? You've never let either Gabriella or Roland taint your life before." Mac understood she might be upset by her mother's press conference, but he had to be honest and point out it was typical Gabriella behaviour. "I actually think it was tame compared to previous instances of attention seeking by Gabriella."

"I guess. She certainly could have made it a lot more sordid."

The knowledge behind Lilli's words made Mac pause, but she continued before he could question her.

"From the minute Lachlan reached eighteen and she knew Dad had started divorce proceedings my wonderful mother has been trying to crawl her way into my brother's bed." Lilli shuddered. "God. The woman disgusts me."

Lilli shot to her feet and charged down the stairs. Mac bounded after her. She'd made it halfway across the yard before he caught up. "Wait. Where are you going?"

"For a swim. I need to cool off."

Mac grabbed her arm and spun her around. "You can't go swimming when you're this upset."

"Upset doesn't begin to describe how I'm feeling about my mother's latest attention-grabbing performance. If I don't get rid of some of this energy, I'm going to do what I've wanted to since I saw Gabriella's little TV appearance."

He pulled her into his arms. "You have every right to be upset but try—"

Lilli pushed from his embrace. "I'm not upset. I'm furious! I'd like to find her and yank out every last bleach-blonde strand on her head!"

She threw her hands in the air and stormed off. Mac watched her go. He'd got it wrong. It wasn't self-pity. It was frustration and anger at the person Lilli should have been able to trust most. How Lilli had turned out normal was beyond him. With parents like hers, she could easily have turned out like Aaron Watson. Pampered and privileged. Instead, she'd built a business, had a successful modelling career and kept friendships from school. He owed her an apology for all the times he'd accused her of being spoilt and selfish.

Sighing, Mac followed Lilli. He reached the edge of the yard just in time to see her strip out of her skirt and enter the water wearing only her skimpy tank top and thong. His heart slammed against his ribs as he glanced up and down the beach. The stretch of sand was private and only accessible to those living along the water's edge, but that didn't mean it was secluded enough for Lilli to swim in her underwear. And with the McDermotts in the spotlight, he wouldn't be surprised if a photographer lurked close by.

God, she was going to be the death of him. If she wasn't making his heart race with arousal she was doing it with fear. One thing Mac was certain of was life with Lilli would never be dull, and up until now his life had been as boring as living in a cardboard box. He glanced down the beach once more. No one was around, but that didn't mean it would stay that way. Lilli continued to swim out deeper. Did he dare?

Mac had done a lot of things out of character in the last twenty-four hours, one more couldn't hurt. With a smile, he unbuttoned his pants and pushed them down. He reached over his head, grabbed his T-shirt and yanked it off. Dressed in only his boxer briefs, he headed for the water and the only woman who could tempt him into the deep end.

9

LILLIAN HEARD Mac splashing as he approached. She'd swum out deep so she could roll to her back and float. The last thing she expected was for Mac to join her in the water. Especially seeing how she knew he wasn't wearing swimmers. She smiled and closed her eyes, waited for him to reach her.

Mac grabbed her ankle and pulled her towards him. "I thought you wanted to swim?"

"I did, but once I got in I changed my mind." She raised her head and opened her eyes. "Are you naked, Mackenzie Harris?"

He threw back his head and laughed.

It wasn't often Mac relaxed and let go. Watching him laugh from deep in his gut did a number on her. She wanted to see him like this all the time. This carefree man willing to strip down and wade into the water with her was normally hidden from view. Lillian decided to make it her mission to bring out this side of Mac. He might not always want to play, but she'd be damned if she'd let him go back inside his shell now that he'd come out.

The cool water flowed over her as she moved around behind him. Plastering herself to his back, she wrapped her arms around him and rested her chin on his shoulder. He was touching bottom so she hooked her legs over his hips and pressed her sex against his back.

"Jesus." A shiver worked its way down his spine, vibrating through her chest. "I can feel your heat. Are you hot for me?"

Lil nipped at his earlobe. "You know I am."

He put his arms behind them and cupped her arse. "I said we weren't going to jump back into bed yet."

She licked his neck, scrapped her teeth over his shoulder. "We're not in bed, Mac."

"Shit." He let her go and, in a move she couldn't follow, had her chest pressed to his and his mouth on hers.

Lost in his kiss, Lil let him lead. He brushed his tongue over her lips, her teeth and finally against hers. Caress after caress, they explored, took and gave. The kiss lacked the desperation of earlier. Instead, it was soft, almost playful. She revelled in the difference, enjoyed this teasing, mischievous side to Mac. Her fingers tangled in his hair as she tugged him closer. Their hips rocked and his erection pressed against her thong, pushing the thin strip of cloth between her folds. Heat and moisture flooded her core and her pussy clenched.

She tore her mouth from his. "Please."

"Not here."

"Why? No one can see."

"Dammit, Lilli, we're in salt water. It's not the best thing to rub into sensitive places." Mac tightened his grip on her back and started walking to shore.

"Where are you going?"

"Inside."

"Please tell me we're going to finish what we started this

time." If he said no, she'd drown him and let his body wash out to sea.

"You couldn't stop me now if you held a gun to my head."

When they reached the sand, Mac put her on her feet, slapped her arse and bent to pick up their discarded clothing. "Get a move on, woman. Shower. My room. Now."

Lillian laughed as she jogged up the beach and across the yard. She detoured to the hot tub where she pulled a couple of towels from the under-bench storage cupboard. She wrapped one around herself and tossed the other to Mac as he came up the stairs.

"Don't drip seawater on the clean floors." Lil briskly rubbed the towel over her body before dropping it to the deck near the door. "I'll come down and grab the wet stuff later. Leave our clothes with the towels."

Mac had dried himself and was in the process of stripping out of his underwear when Lil entered the house. If she got too close or a good look at him they'd never make it upstairs, so she quickened her pace. Her wet top clung to her breasts and her thong rubbed over her clit with each step she took. She'd be lucky if she didn't climax before she got halfway up the stairs. She should have removed her clothes at the back door as Mac had. The gentle rub might have been pleasurable at first, but the farther she walked the harsher the friction became. Suddenly, Mac's earlier warning about salt water made sense.

She reached Mac's room and headed straight for the shower. With the rasping of her underwear against her sensitive flesh barely tolerable any longer, Lil immediately stripped out of the wet thong and kicked it aside. Leaning into the shower recess, she switched on the water before removing her top. Mac came in behind her and slipped his arms around her waist. He pulled her back until her body was flush with his. His hands slid up her stomach to cup her breasts and she arched her spine, driving her hardening nipples into his palms.

"Damn, it feels good to get my hands on you," Mac whispered in her ear before he scraped his teeth down the side of her neck.

Lillian moaned as Mac's mouth blazed a trail of hot kisses over her shoulder and down her spine. He lavished attention on each bump, each hollow, as he worked his way lower. Reversing direction, Mac danced his lips back to her shoulder and finally her nape, where he proceeded to drive her wild with nips and licks. A shiver travelled the length of her body, tightening her thighs and curling her toes.

"You like that?" Mac murmured against her skin before repeating his mind-numbing caresses.

"Mmm." Lil could only hum. Her brain couldn't form words never mind get her vocal cords to work.

"We're going to forget last night happened, Lilli." He tugged on her earlobe with his teeth. "We're going to pretend this is your first time and I'm going to do it right, do everything you deserve and more."

She wanted to protest his words. Wanted to tell him last night was the best of her life, but he distracted her by pinching her nipples between fingers and thumbs. Rolling. Tugging. Plucking. A moan slipped over her lips as he continued to tease the sensitive nubs while suckling the delicate skin beneath her ear.

"You taste like Lilli with a pinch of salt," he spoke between kisses. The words vibrated across her flesh, sent a burst of tingles in all directions.

"Mac." His name left her throat on a sigh.

He slowed his strokes and his touch went from teasing to soothing. She should have been disappointed, should have whimpered in complaint, but Mac had changed the tempo of his lips and hands, stirring her in a different way. An easy climb to the peak instead of a mad dash.

"Water's warm. In you get." Mac's hands gripped her waist and he lifted off the floor and into the shower. "Careful. Don't slip."

He moved in behind her, turning her around so he took the full force of the spray. And then the real seduction began. Starting with her hair, Mac worked his way from top to bottom, washing and rinsing until no part of her body held a trace of salt or sand. Lil closed her eyes and leaned into him. She couldn't remember anyone ever showing her such care, and Mac had done it twice in the last twenty-four hours. If she hadn't already been in love with the man, she'd have fallen right here.

With each brush of his soap-slicked hands, Lil gave a little more of her soul. She'd known all along that Mac was the one for her, but knowing something was meant to be and making it happen were two different things. She hadn't been stupid enough to believe love could conquer all. Still wasn't. They might have both accepted the change in their relationship but they had to make it work in the real world yet.

"Stop thinking," Mac whispered in her ear. "We'll get back to the real world later."

"Will we?"

"Yes." He spun her around to face him, his arms slid around her waist, his hands cupping her arse. "For now it's just you and me."

He lowered his head, drawing his mouth closer to hers, and Lil gave in. She pushed to her toes and met him halfway. They'd make this work. They had to. Because now that she knew what it was like to love Mac freely, she wanted to spend every day for the rest of her life doing it.

MAC KISSED Lilli with everything he had. She drove him crazy just by breathing, and yet he couldn't get enough of her. He wanted a do-over for last night. Wanted to give her a first time she'd never forget. And while he couldn't turn back the clock, what he could do was give pleasure so great she forgot all about the night before. Forgot every other touch. He'd make sure he was the only one she remembered.

He stroked his tongue over hers, teased and taunted until she softened against him. And when she did, he demanded more. Her arms were wrapped around his neck, her fingers tangled in his hair and her glorious breasts pressed into his chest, her nipples hard and pointy. They weren't the only hard thing either. His cock, caught between their bodies, throbbed. But he wouldn't be getting release anytime soon. This was about Lilli.

Easing back, he changed the angle of his mouth on hers. He licked at her lips, sucked the bottom one into his mouth and nipped it with his teeth. The moan that slipped from her throat sent a thrill through his blood, flooding his veins with hunger. She pushed higher on her toes and rocked into him, her sex cradling his, bathing him with wet heat. They had to slow down or he'd take her against the wall with the water pouring over them. Not what he pictured for a do-over of her first time.

Separating their mouths, he trailed kisses across her cheek to her ear. "Time to change location."

"Huh?" She melted against him.

Mac smiled. Satisfaction thrummed through him when he looked at Lilli's lust-dazed state. Switching off the shower, he said, "Come on. Time to hop out."

He stepped back, taking her with him. Mac grabbed a towel, wrapped it around her shoulders and tugged her close for a quick kiss. As usual, her lips proved too much temptation, and he soon found himself lost in the dark recesses of her mouth. Pulling back, he gasped for air and wondered if she would always be this much of an addiction. How he'd lived this long without kissing her, touching her, he hadn't a clue, and he had no intention of finding out if he could survive without her from now on either.

She smiled up at him. A dreamy haze clouded her eyes, and Mac had never seen anything more beautiful in his life. Yes, she'd graced numerous fashion magazines, even been named Australia's sexiest woman, but nothing compared to the sight before him. Her eyes sparkled with a mixture of desire, love and happiness. It was the last emotion that delivered the blow to his gut. He'd made her happy. If fate saw fit to end his life now, he'd die satisfied knowing he'd given that to her. But life wouldn't be that cruel, not when he had plenty more to offer the woman in his arms.

"Now who's thinking too much?" She slid her hand up over his chest and onto his face where she cupped his jaw. "Take me to bed, Mac."

Who could deny a request like that? Certainly not him. He scooped her up into his arms, carried her to his bed and laid her down. He followed her, aligning his body with hers so they touched from shoulder to feet. Her legs parted and he settled himself between them. Their bodies, still wet, slid together with ease when he rocked against her. Lilli's back arched, her pussy cradling his erection within its moist folds. Mac groaned. Rocked again and again, driving them both higher with each stroke.

"Mac," she breathed his name.

He wanted to hold back. Wanted to give her more pleasure than she ever imagined possible, but she moved against him, pulled him deeper with every roll of her hips. Every brush of her hand. She was seducing him. With her demand. Her surrender. With every breath she took, he lost a little more of his mind. His heart. And he gave them willingly.

"Please, Mac."

Lilli wrapped her legs around his waist and tilted her hips. His cock slipped through her folds and lodged in her opening. One flex and he could be buried to the hilt, but he held back. He grabbed her arms and pinned them to the bed beside her. Twining his fingers through hers, he held them in place.

"Look at me." He waited for her to open her eyes. "I want to see you when I give you what you want."

Her gaze rose to meet his and he sucked in a breath at the depth of emotion flashing out at him. Mac locked his eyes on hers and pushed inside. He buried his cock in a long, slow thrust. Balls deep, he held tight, kept his hips pressed to hers and savoured the sensations surrounding him. Like a hot, wet fist, she gripped him, the slick walls of her pussy coating his length from root to tip. She bucked beneath him and he withdrew until her entrance once again encircled his crown.

"Again," Lilli demanded.

He did as she asked. Lunging forward, he sank slowly inside her heat before retreating once more, making sure to slide his shaft over her clit with each stroke.

"Again." She rocked against him.

Mac kept his eyes on hers and he gave her all he had. He surged in and out, keeping the pace even until the pleasure became too much but not enough. Lilli writhed under him as she sought relief. Her movements drove him higher, pushed him faster. Harder. Before long, the leisurely tempo turned frantic and they barrelled towards the edge with desperate need.

"Mac!"

She clamped around him, her pussy convulsing in wave

after wave of release. He clenched his jaw, fought to keep from coming before he experienced the full force of Lilli's orgasm. But it was too much. The power of her contracting muscles sliced through his control and sucked the come right out of him. Spasm after spasm rocked him. His back arched as he slammed his cock to the hilt once more and stayed there. Buried deep, Mac poured himself inside her as a cry tore from his throat. "Lilli."

"WELL, that didn't go to plan."

Lil smiled. "I'm not complaining."

"Good. I'm not sure I could offer you a do-over right now."

She laughed. "You're off the hook for now."

"Excellent." Mac threw his arm over her stomach and pulled her against his chest. "Wake me in a week."

Snuggling closer, she tucked her head beneath his chin. "Not sure I'll be up by then."

"Fine by me." He gave her a squeeze. "I'd be happy to stay just like this forever."

"Mmm, me too."

Lillian lay curled against Mac's side and listened as his breathing slowed. She wouldn't say he was snoring exactly, but it was close. As tired as she was sleep eluded her so she stayed tucked beside a sleeping Mac and thought about what the next few weeks would bring.

Her perfume didn't launch for another month but there were still a lot of things to sort out ready for release day. Lilli Pond's winter range had gone on sale weeks ago and already the figures were looking good. More than good. Other than the final Golden Lilli campaign ads to approve, she had a clear schedule. And then there was Mac. She wasn't sure where or how they'd fit together but she was more than ready to make it work.

"Stop thinking." Mac's sleepy voice startled her.

"I can't help it."

"You know I'm not going anywhere, right?"

"Yes."

"Good. Now go to sleep. You'll need your energy."

"Why?"

"You still owe me a date."

EPILOGUE

SIX DAYS later

A date. They were going on a date. Lil couldn't hold back the smile as she put the final touches on her makeup. The last week had been the most unsettling and contented of her life, and Mackenzie Harris had been the centre of it. While they'd carried on their everyday lives, each going to work as though nothing had changed. It had. Both their worlds had shifted. Or maybe it was more appropriate to say their paths had finally converged. There had been only one hiccup.

Lachlan.

Her brother hadn't returned home until Monday, and when he did it was to punch Mac in the face and turn right around and leave again. She'd tried to call him, but Lachlan hadn't answered any of her calls, or returned them. Thank God for Cam. Her friend had willingly spilled the beans and said her brother just needed time to adjust to her and Mac's new relationship. Add Mac's assurance that everything would be okay and she had to believe that. If anyone knew Lachlan and his thought processes it was Mac. She trusted him with her heart, she could trust him about her brother.

But not even the worry over her brother could dampen her happiness. She'd been floating on air since Mac had rung and asked her out. He'd told her to be ready by seven and dress casual. When she'd pressed for details, he'd said he wanted to surprise her and quickly ended the call. Lil had thought about ringing back but then the excitement had taken hold. She was dating Mackenzie Harris. Her mouth had been in a permanent upward curve all week, but this evening's agenda had her flashing her pearly white smile in blinding intensity.

Her outfit—a miniskirt and tank top—were designed to taunt and tease. The mini was black leather, soft and supple, it clung to her curves like skin. Lil turned her head to check out her rear view in the mirror. Oh yeah, like skin. She gave her arse a little wiggle and thought about driving Mac wild with the sway of her hips. He'd proven to have a thing for her arse. When they were together, he always found a reason to smooth his hand over the taut curves she didn't need to work hard to maintain.

"God bless good DNA." Lil twirled around to get the full view. The tank hugged her breasts, the neck scooping low to reveal a decent amount of cleavage, and she tilted forward to make sure she wouldn't fall out. Tempting Mac was one thing, exposing herself in public another. Satisfied her modesty was safe, Lil turned one full circle, craning her neck to see from every angle.

"Damn. Mac is gonna swallow his tongue."

Grinning, Lil packed away her makeup and headed downstairs to wait. In her overexcited state she'd managed to be ready early. And that was after dragging her heals as long as she could. Sighing, she made her way to the kitchen where she'd set up her laptop to work on the Golden Lilli campaign and Lilli

Pond's summer collection. With at least an hour to kill, she pulled up the business plan for Calla, the women's range of evening wear she planned to launch in eighteen months.

No. Not even Lachlan's silence and obvious disapproval could douse Lil's satisfaction. She'd achieved so much, hoped to do more in the near future and her most wished for fantasy had become reality. Lillian McDermott had a date with Mackenzie Harris.

MAC PICKED up his briefcase and laid it on his desk. Popping the locks, he opened it and began loading in the files he planned to work on over the weekend. He hadn't planned on taking any work home, but Lilli had told him she had to work Saturday morning, so he'd work instead of moping around the house waiting for her to return.

"Hey, you leaving?" Lachlan stuck his head into Mac's office.

"Yeah." Mac held his breath. They'd worked together all week without trouble, but they still hadn't talked about him and Lilli.

"Mind if I hitch a ride?"

"Where's your car?"

"Cam dropped me off after I took the bike in for repairs."

Mac wasn't sure what had thawed his friend's icy attitude, but he wasn't about to ask. "Sure. I'm leaving in ten."

"I'll meet you in the garage."

"Okay."

He stood staring at the doorway after Lachlan left. Mac didn't hold a grudge about the punch his friend had thrown. He figured if it were him in Lachlan's shoes and his best mate was screwing with his baby sister he'd have done the same. But now that Lachlan had gotten that out of his system they needed to talk. No time better than being confined in a car for sixty minutes. Mac finished loading his bag and switched off his computer. He grabbed his briefcase and phone and headed out.

When Mac exited the lift in the parking garage, Lachlan was leaning against his BMW. Neither of them spoke when they got in the car. They'd spent forty minutes in the peak-hour rush with thousands of others in a hurry to get the weekend started before Lachlan broke the silence.

"About Monday."

Stopped in traffic, Mac glanced over at his friend. "Already forgotten."

"I appreciate that, but every time I think of you and Lilli—together—I want to punch you all over again." Lachlan stared straight ahead, not once making eye contact.

Mac could see the muscle in Lachlan's jaw twitching and knew they needed to get past this or risk losing a lifetime's friendship. "I love her, Lachlan."

"Yeah, I get that." Lachlan dragged a hand down his face before finally turning to face Mac. "Look. I'll get my head around it. Eventually. And if I'm honest, and I'd like to think we haven't lost that, then I have to say if anyone's going to be screwing around with my sister I want to know I can trust them."

"Sticking with honesty, I have to admit to wanting her for years. Our friendship, yours and mine, has been the barrier to me pursuing Lilli."

A horn honked behind them and Mac turned to see the light had changed and traffic was moving again. "And I'm not screwing around."

"You're telling me you're not having sex?"

Mac laughed as he manoeuvred his car through traffic. "Somehow I doubt you want me to actually answer that."

Lachlan groaned. "You're right. Don't answer that. Shit. That's an image I don't need."

The tension inside him eased. Things weren't completely ironed out, but Mac had no doubt that once Lachlan got used to the idea of him and Lilli as a couple they'd be back on solid ground again. He decided a change of subject might help. "I take it things are better with Cameron."

"We're getting there. She's nothing like I expected and better than any fantasy I ever conjured up as a teenager." Mac could hear the pleasure in Lachlan's voice.

"I take it that's where you've been staying all week." Mac glanced in his side mirror and changed lanes.

"I wanted to be on hand in case the press decided her fence was not a deterrent."

"Now they've got something else to spend time on things should calm down."

"Nice work getting those shots of Aaron Watson going into the rehab clinic, by the way."

"He owed me. And it's not like his alcohol problem is a big secret. Last I heard he'd signed a deal with a mag for an exclusive on his story when he's out."

"Jesus. Anything for publicity."

"We probably shouldn't knock it seeing how the media is what puts money in our bank accounts." Mac smiled as he turned into their suburb.

"After this past weekend, I'll be more than happy to stay on my side of the media fence."

"You and me both," Mac agreed.

They fell silent as Mac drove through the quiet suburban streets. Unlike earlier, it didn't hold that razor edge of tension. The closer they got to the house the less strained the air between them became. As he turned onto their street, the muscles in Mac's gut loosened and he knew they'd be okay. It might take a while, but he had no doubt he and Lachlan would be fine. Just like he and Lilli would be. Thinking of Lilli brought a smile to his face.

He had a date.

Mac couldn't remember the last time he'd gone out on a date or when he'd anticipated one as much as tonight. He'd planned a simple evening. They'd eat at a small pizzeria that, in his opinion, served the best pizza in Sydney. Then they'd either take a walk on the beach or catch a movie. Lilli could choose that part of their date. And when the night was over, he'd bring her home and kiss her at the door. Of course he'd follow her in after, but he wanted the traditional date, the sweet courtship they missed by fighting their feelings for so long.

It was no wonder they'd come together in a blinding flash. A person could only live in denial for so long, and Mac was extremely pleased they were past that. They couldn't go back and change the past, but they could certainly change the future. And he planned to make the most of every day he had. Starting with tonight.

"Why aren't you pulling into the garage?" Lachlan asked.

"Because I'm going straight back out." Mackenzie parked his BMW at the curb and switched off the engine.

"Jesus. You could at least pull into the driveway," his friend grumbled.

"Nope. Need to park it on the street for this to work." Mac removed his keys and got out. He was halfway up the walk before Lachlan caught up.

"That's the last time I hitch a ride from work with you."

"Noted." They reached the front door and Mac pressed the bell.

"What the fuck are you doing?"

"Ringing the bell."

"You live here, dickhead. Use your key."

"Can't."

"Why? Did you lose it again?"

Mac turned to face Lachlan. "As I recall it was *you* who lost the house key, and I have to ring the bell. I'm taking Lilli out on a date. That requires ringing the bell."

"A date? You're kidding?"

"Does it look or sound like I'm kidding?"

Lachlan eyed him before rolling his eyes. "Man, you two are weird. You seeing my sister is bad enough, but this is just plain screwy."

"Nope. This is two people building a life together from the ground up."

"This isn't helping me decide how I feel about you and my sister."

"It doesn't matter how you feel. What matters is how Lilli feels."

"Jeez, you've got it bad."

Mac smiled as the door opened and Lilli stood there in a miniskirt and tank top.

"Oh, yeah. I've got it bad."

Truth Or Dare

By Rhian Cahill

Sometimes it takes a daring heart to find true love

Even at an exclusive party, Miki Drummond finds herself retreating to a safe corner. Watching life go by is something she does well, especially after the hell of her collapsed marriage.

The last thing she expected to do was 'bump' into not one but two blasts from her high school past.

Best friends, Grant Rogers and Dayne Pierce never forgot Miki—ever—and a game of Truth or Dare seems like the perfect way to get reacquainted. Except Miki repeatedly chooses to take a shot rather than reveal her obvious pain, but neither man is willing to let her hide in the past for long.

With Grant and Dayne, Miki is caught in an electrically charged moment that offers her sweet torment and unimaginable pleasure.

But one night of pure fantasy is all Miki dares to take until her two lovers dare her to accept the hard truth. Walking away is no longer an option.

Note: If you find yourself sandwiched between two hunky men...it might be worth taking the dare.

http://www.rhiancahill.com/books/party-games/truth-or-dare/

Miki rolled over with a groan, her whole body throbbed like a rock band at Big Day Out. Her mouth was dry and her tongue and lips felt swollen. Her eyes refused to open, the heavy weight of her lids too much for her tired muscles to lift. Every part of her ached like she'd been run over by the nine-fifteen train. Lying perfectly still, she tried to focus on where she was and recall what the hell she'd done the night before that might warrant such agony this morning, but the last thing Miki remembered was sitting down with Dayne and Grant—

Air rushed into her lungs on a harsh gasp.

She hadn't?

The muffled snore that came from Miki's left made her flinch. She didn't move, didn't breathe. Squeezing her eyes tight on the memories now flooding her mind, she hoped it was all a drunken dream and dared to wish it wasn't. A snore tore through the room on her right and Mikaila cringed. One eye popped open and she turned her head first left, then right, a quick glance on either side before squeezing both eyes closed so tight she could feel the sting of tears.

Oh my God, she *had*.

Her heart raced and she struggled to draw in a breath. Heat crawled up her face, no doubt the accompanying red tinge with it. Could she be any more mortified? Miki tried to calm herself. Both her bed buddies were sleeping soundly if their snoring was anything to go by, so all she had to do was slip out from between them, grab her clothes and make a run for it. Easier said than done when she had no idea where her clothes had ended up. She swallowed over the lump in her throat, and as slow as possible so as not to shake the bed, she inched her way down the mattress.

The blankets had long since been pushed from the bed so nothing obstructed her progress until she got about halfway. Dizziness stopped her. Miki gasped for air. She hadn't realised she'd been holding her breath. It was the second gust of oxygen to her lungs that threatened to bring her undone. Breathing through her nose coated her nostrils with the scent of hot male flesh and sex. Her insides clenched and moisture pooled in her pussy, seeped out to cover her folds. She licked her lips, the taste of them still on her tongue. Memories of what they'd done were fresh in her mind and sent lust licking through her veins.

Her pulse sped up with renewed arousal. How she could possibly be horny after all they'd done was beyond her, but that was the least of her worries. She needed to get out of here. Away from the enticing scent of Dayne and Grant before she did something stupid like crawl back up the bed and wake them. Wriggling until her arse hit the edge of the mattress and her feet touched the floor, Miki paused, waited to see if her movements had woken either man. When neither stirred, she pushed herself upright and looked around for her clothes.

Her underwear lay about five feet away but there was no sign of her bra or dress. Miki picked up a blanket from the mess of bedclothes on the floor and wrapped it around her shoulders. She tip-toed to her undies and scooped them up. Balling them in her hand, she surveyed the room once more before remembering they'd removed her dress in the other room. Deciding to go without her bra, she padded her way to the door and slipped out into the hall. She quickened her pace as she headed for the movie room. Once inside, she dropped the blanket and pulled on her dress and panties.

It wasn't until she reached the front door that Miki realised she had no shoes and Frankie had her house key and money. Backtracking to look for a phone, she tried not to make any noise. The last thing she wanted was to get caught sneaking out of the house like a thief. Spying a phone on the kitchen wall, she raced over, lifted the receiver and dialled Frankie's home number.

"Come on, come on. Pick up, Frankie."

After the tenth ring, Mikaila gave up and tried Frankie's cell. Again there was no answer, and when voice mail kicked in Miki hung up. What the hell would she say?

Come get me, I'm at Dayne and Grant's place 'cause I spent the morning having the best sex of my life with two men I've secretly lusted after since high school?

Frankie would probably whoop for joy and pat her on the back. Miki closed her eyes and leaned her forehead against the wall, the last twelve hours replaying in her mind. Taking deep breaths, she struggled to understand what she'd done and why she thought sneaking out this morning was such a good idea.

She'd never dreamed being with them would be so good. All her fantasies paled into nothing when compared to the real thing. There'd been no awkwardness either, their love making, no, the *sex* had been natural, as if the three of them had done it a million times before. And the orgasms had blown every other climax she'd ever had out of the water too. Everything about their night together was perfect, so why was she running this morning?

Both Grant and Dayne had told her they wanted more than one night, but she didn't know what that entailed or if she wanted to know. The thought of not seeing them again had her chest tightening and her stomach cramping, but could they turn fantasy into reality? She'd never run from anything in the past, never been a quitter. Her long drawn-out marriage was proof of that. If last night had been a mistake then she'd face it and move on. And if not, she'd deal with the hurdles that came her way, but there was no way she would be a coward and run.

Mikaila pushed off the wall and turned in the direction of the hall. It was time to tell some truths and possibly take the biggest dare of her life.

http://www.rhiancahill.com/books/party-games/truth-or-dare/

ABOUT THE AUTHOR

Rhian Cahill is the alter ego of a former stay-at-home mother of four. With motherly duties rapidly dwindling Rhian is able to make use of the fertile imagination she used to keep herself sane for all those years of slavery. Having spent years living overseas and visiting tropical climates has helped inspire some steamy stories.

Multi-published in erotic romance and contemporary romance, Rhian, with the help of Mr. Muse, spends her days and nights writing.

When not glued to the keyboard you'll find her book or knitting in hand avoiding any and all housework as much as possible.

For more on Rhian –

Website – http://www.rhiancahill.com/
Newsletter signup – http://www.rhiancahill.com/contact/newsletter/
Reader group - https://www.facebook.com/groups/211469429208895/
Twitter – https://twitter.com/RhianCahill
FaceBook – https://www.facebook.com/RhianCahillAuthor
Instagram – http://instagram.com/rhiancahill/
BookBub – https://www.bookbub.com/authors/rhian-cahill
Goodreads page - https://www.goodreads.com/rhian_cahill

LOOK FOR THESE TITLES BY RHIAN CAHILL

Doing Logan

Shut Up And Kiss Me

Secret Confessions: Sydney Housewives – Virginia

Boys Of Summer

Bondi Beach Boys

Sand, Surf And Sunnie

Holiday Romances

Christmas Wishes

New Year's Kisses

Valentine's Dates

Secret Santa

Passport To Passion Collection

One Night In Bangkok

Singapore Fling

Coyote Hunger Series

Coyote Home – Book 1

Coyote Wild – Book 2

Coyote Whispers – Book 3

Coyote Law – Book 3.5

Coyote Lies – Book 4

Only You Series

All Of You – Book 1

Party Games Series

Truth Or Dare

Spin The Bottle

Pass The Parcel – Novella

Are You Game Series

7 Minutes In Heaven – Book 1

Catch'n'Kiss – Book 2

Red Light, Green Light – Book 3

Frosty's Snowmen Series

A Touch Of Frost

A Kiss From Kringle

A Taste For Kandy

Hearts Are Wild Series

No More Talking (novella)

Dare You To (novella)

Mad Love

Winter Lake Series

Love Me Like You Do

Love The Way You Are

When You Love Someone

Let me Love You

Wild Rush Of Love

For a full list of Rhian's available books visit her website

http://www.rhiancahill.com/books/